CAPTURED

DIRTY FAIRY TALES SERIES: ENEMIES TO LOVERS ROMANCE (DEMANDING DADDY BOOK 1)

OLIVIA FOX

This is all fiction. No one who is getting down with one another is related. All sexual acts are between consenting adults and if there is no talk of condoms, birth control, etc. it's only because it's **fiction and fantasy**. If you are having sex, here are some essential resources:

PREP REDUCED THE CHANCE OF CONTRACTING HIV BY 99%

HTTPS://WWW.CDC.GOV/HIV/BASICS/PREP.HTML

GET TESTED - FIND OUT WHY YOU SHOULD

HTTPS://WWW.MAYOCLINIC.ORG/DISEASES-CONDITIONS/SEXUALLY-TRANSMITTED-DISEASES-STDS/IN-DEPTH/STD-TESTING/ART-20046019

Hi Kitten,

Get my book *Branded by Daddy* ABSOLUTELY FREE when you subscribe to my newsletter. YES! Gimme me my book! I need it so badly: https://BookHip.com/ZSNNJG

Come join the private VIP group for fans of Olivia Fox. It's a gathering place for readers who love best-selling books with naughty-but-nice, alpha males, Daddy Doms and stories with spank. Plus find out about advanced reader copies and more!

Foxy Fan VIP Group:

https://www.facebook.com/groups/1829265110510385/

BELLA

Sacramento, California
The Dive Bar

I parked myself on the bar stool, back stooped, holding my chin tucked to my chest to cover my face with the brim of a black baseball hat that said "I can't people today." The vibe I meant to lay down was *don't talk to me.*

The bass beat filled the air around my head, cuffing my eardrums with occasional pressure while I checked out the front door for assassins. The disco lights mopped the dance floor every few minutes, displaying sticky, spilled drinks in overlapping, translucent layers. It was too shadowy to see properly.

Exactly the point.

No one working from a photograph would recognize me beneath this imperfect lighting. There was an untouched shot of tequila, to keep up appearances, in front of me. I picked it up and rolled it between my palms and wondered how it would sound if I threw it against the back-lit bottles of booze arranged like ornaments on the racks behind the bartender. How many people in this room were holding shot-glass-throwing feelings beneath their skin and stifling their unrest with booze?

The prospect was unnerving. I searched around to check for hooligans again.

The Dive Bar had its charms and appeared to be free of knuckle draggers for the moment, full of young people liquoring themselves up to dance and inspecting the area for potential hook ups. I'd been here thirty minutes, to avoid going stir crazy in my room. Left to my own devices, I could make myself miserable in a matter of seconds, using only my brain.

It was only humanly possible to pick apart at computer security systems for so long, and I had been at it all day. So it was a welcome distraction to hear patrons chat about the fact that the human aquarium overhead cost one-point-five-million dollars. Let's hope that price tag made the tank structurally intact.

Being "on the run" was surreal. I knew I needed to keep moving—that the same characters who needed to locate my dad figured that I was just the person to point them in his general direction. They were mistaken. My dad was too smart to be traceable via cell phone or computer. His last communication let me know he was fleeing the country and would be back when he had ample proof to put Bunker Inc. away for good.

And he told me: "Run."

The line between ethical hacking and just plain hacking was a fine one. Papa and I both served clients who hired us to break into their computer network, find security vulnerabilities, and suggest solutions. While doing a job he was paid to do, he discovered abnormal activities, which incriminated Bunker Inc., a corporation worth millions. Whenever I thought of the thugs that were after my dad, they appeared as cartoon characters in my mind. Pinstripe suit. Black fedora with a flashy baby blue band. A five o'clock shadow covering the chin and lower cheeks in a broad stripe. Heavy black stripes staining the brow, like shoe polish swiped over pencil-dot pupils. Eyes surrounded by dark, sagging circles, with a round nose. And two ham-sized hands, curled into angry fists. It was better to think of them as comical. Easier to escape cartoonish goons than the evil and clever masterminds who controlled their puppet strings from behind the respectable screen of their company.

My fear needed damping down. I could feel my shoulders tighten and my legs shake where I had them perched on the rungs of the bar stool.

I found gangster movies soothing. "My circle is small. I'm loyal as hell. Never fuck me over." (*Scarface*). The leading characters lived with horse heads in their beds; dead, or semi-dead bodies in the trunks of their cars; poison in their cannoli. Their torment made my life simple and solvable by comparison.

Until it wasn't.

Now here I was sitting under the human mermaid tank, wishing to go on undiscovered in the gloomy light and disconcerting dance music decibel. Being on the run was one way to have an adventure. All my life, I'd kept my head in books, escaping reality, yearning for the day when I could seek excitement of my own. And now that day has come.

The mermaids and mermen showed off spinning slow somersaults above cocktail-sipping patrons who ignored their fin propelled antics. The swimming creatures kept my attention. I saw a faint, blue-green scaled tail propel from the far end of the tank to above where I was sitting. Its owner plucked out a mirror and silver comb from a wooden chest at the bottom of the container and combed the long blond tresses of her hair, which floated diaphanously above her. When would she take a breath? How long could she hold it?

I counted. I got to forty-five seconds when I was interrupted by some dude in a black leather motorcycle jacket who plunked himself on the stool next to me. "New in town?" I got that instinctual sense that skittered across the back of my shoulders like a daddy long-leg spider. "Buy you a drink?" He perched his feet on the bar stool and jiggled his knees, drumming his fingers on his acne scarred chin.

"No, thanks; I'm all set." I crossed my arms against my breasts.

"Oh, come on, that's no way to make friends." He sidled his barstool closer to mine, and I slid my hand into my right pocket, wrapping my fingers around the comforting shape of my pepper spray. You can never be too careful. Especially when trying to avoid being captured by goons.

There was a deep, rumbling voice behind me, "Hey Bud, she said she wasn't interested. Besides, she's with me. You wanna get off *my* stool?"

I sure as shit was not with anyone, male or female, let alone an hombre with the voice of Barry White and the manners of a caveman.

"If the two of you don't mind, I'll just be seeing myself out; thank you very much." I still hadn't turned around to see the source of that oh-so-jagged sound, the kind that threaded through feminine parts like liquid longing.

Hot. Sexy. Even if you weren't thinking about licking him, the noise would wind your biological clock to ticking speed.

Suddenly, the shot of tequila in front of me was tempting. *Burn away the lustful feels. Send them back into the closet where they've been hiding since...well, since ever.*

I refused to turn around—no matter what. I'd toss back

the Cuervo and head back to my hotel. But the skeevy guy on my left butt in on that plan with his exit.

"I, I, ah meant no harm. I'll just be on my way. I don't want to intrude on your date."

That libido-licking voice again. "Excellent choice." He took his place next to me and placed his IPA on the counter next to my shot of tequila; a beer drinking Goliath settling in next to his giantess. I noticed he wasn't touching his drink either.

Sweet heavenly sprocket. He had gladiator arms and a sailor's ink. Okay if seamen turned you on, I guess.

Not my type at all. A far cry from Mr. Darcy, Heathcliff, or Atticus Finch: the gentleman heroes that fueled my fantasy.

Try telling that to my quivering hoo-ha. I felt my pulse right between my legs, hotter than it had a right to be, and I wriggled on my seat to ease the pressure of my jeans against my lady bits.

His bulging biceps were nothing in comparison to his granite jaw and angel lips, which I admired while sneaking a sidelong glance at him. If a stone statue of a messenger of God came to life, it would have the mouth of this man. Strong lips, frozen almost in pout. The sheer size of them put Angelina Jolie's pucker to shame, and my mind began to wander down the path of what was possible to achieve with lips like those.

Kiss.

Nibble.

Suck.

No distractions! You're on the run. Don't forget it for even a second.

Vigilance. He may be a bad guy.

"You should be more careful with strange men." His stern scolding made me implode and crumple inward. I just met him and this warrior's disapproval crushed me in its hand.

"I'm sorry; aren't *you* a strange man?" With that, I tossed back my shot of tequila and waved goodbye at the bathing beauty who was fluttering her hands at her sides in the tank above me. An elegant and tiny trail of bubbles trickled out of her nostril. I felt connected to her, even though we hadn't spoken a word.

"That's not what I meant. I'll do you no harm!" His protest was inappropriately loud, such that people noticed and looked our way.

Suddenly, this abrasive stranger scared me. "Well, thanks for coming to my rescue. I've gotta be on my way." I hopped off the bar stool, pushed my way through the pelvis-thrusting dancers, wondering if Mr. Make-Me-Ache liked to dance, and turned around one last time to admire his throw-me-on-the-bed forearms. The left side of his face lit up under the strobe light which blinked with forced festivity. My mouth fell open and my hand flew to my chest at the same moment he turned to slam his stare into mine. Terrible scars covered this side of his face, and his hairline was unnaturally receded like something you would see on a Halloween monster mask.

Oh crap.

He caught me staring. I gaped at him like a rude guppy.

Spinning around and stepping onto the rainbow-colored spots shining from above, I followed them like a garden path, and walked out into the hot summer air. Sacramento summer. It was always at least a hundred degrees.

I needed to get out of there fast and back to safety. The Benton Hotel was only two blocks away from The Dive. It was stupid of me to leave my room in the first place. I recognized the brick wall that led me here but confusion filled my head when I thought of how to get back. The night time air churned around me. My feet took swerving steps of their own accord, as if following the path of a snake, and my eyelids lowered like an automatic garage door. It was impossible to hold them open. They closed, and for the last time I heard that unmistakable voice behind me. I fell into his arms, avoiding the splat of my head on the pavement.

The last thing I made out before letting my eyes flutter shut for was that spark-my-inner-sex-pot voice of his. "Too easy."

LIAM

The despicable privilege of living through hell is knowing that you can.

Five years post-Iraq and this current job was taking candy from a baby. Not only that, but my captive was easy on the eye.

Escaping from an M1Abrams tank fire with half my face intact meant I could survive anything. The punk in his black leather jacket posed no threat, not by a long shot. I could smell his fear despite the dead animal he wore on his back as a tough-guy disguise. It didn't conceal shit. The way he jiggled his knee even as he attempted to hit on the smoking hot female; my escapee. This was a guy who moved through life scared shitless, and I was a dude who wasn't scared of shit.

Place your bets.

Luck is what happens when preparation meets opportunity, and this guy wasn't at all ready for the perfect fucking storm that was coming his way. I rested with my back against the wall for a minute, and could feel the bass beat thumping at my shoulder blades, warning me that frightened animals could be as treacherous as the most powerful in the jungle. His wish to assert dominance over someone, anyone, to prove he wasn't as weak as he looked oozed out of his pores like perspiration. His lack of self-confidence made him willing to prove himself in inappropriate ways.

Like the way he tried to lay his arm over her shoulder, uninvited. The way he still pushed when she said she wasn't interested. These impulses of his might turn ugly, in a private setting where I wasn't standing at his back, blocking him from exerting his will.

My pulse quickened and with clenched teeth, I tapped him on the shoulder when he moved his stool closer to hers. I anchored my hand on my hip when he jumped and reemphasized that the lady wasn't interested. A bully can't abide meeting someone of equal or greater strength. Nine times out of ten, a bully is a coward in disguise. Sure enough, he scuttled away from us like a crab back under its rock, and disappeared into the crowd on the dance floor. I took my place next to her.

When she spoke, it felt like warm massage oil pouring over my cock. The thought of her stroking me with oil chased every coherent thought from my brain and drove all the blood to my groin. I hadn't ever been this greedy for a woman.

Sure, I relieved certain biological urges at the BDSM club, scratching an itch at the only social place I ever visited. I knew how I looked. For that reason it was easier to stick to myself, the only exception being the fugitives I was paid to go after. Also, the extremely occasional trip to the club where I didn't expect more than a sexual encounter. I wanted nothing more. Women liked my brawn. My discipline. And there were ladies in the club who considered my burns a turn on, others who asked me to wear a mask. When it came to kink, it took all kinds.

I hadn't reacted to the sheer presence, the simple sound of a female since...since I couldn't remember. This girl would not welcome me with open arms.

For a moment, I considered walking away.

But I was a professional hired to do a job, and I didn't shirk on my duties. No matter that my dick was conflicted as hell.

There were several close calls with IEDs overseas, but I still had my equipment. Right now there was the jumbo-sized reminder between my legs, a sign it had been a long, dry spell since my last visit to the club and this female at my side was a painful reminder of my prolonged sexual abstinence.

Battle taught me how to read a man same as one dog sniffing another to assess threat level. Battle made me grateful for everyday things. A cock that worked. I knew guys that had theirs blown off or damaged to the point of dysfunction. The club served one purpose: sexual relief. The soothing rainfall sound of her voice made me feel something else. I wanted to possess her, and my heart pounded in my chest at the thought.

I never tied longing to a specific female. This felt like taking off in a C17 cargo plane. My stomach plummeted every time she spoke. Just my luck, the first female to command my every senses' attention—I couldn't stop thinking about smelling her, touching her, licking her—was my ticket to making more on one job than I did in a year.

In spite of my appearance, I *was* a gentleman. My mama raised me right and I knew better than to stare, but what my mama never warned me about is that there would be a girl like this one whose very existence would crush my manners under her tiny foot.

Do your duty, Whittaker. They're paying you to catch her, not wonder how small her hand would be in yours.

The yearning got worse when I followed her outside and watched as her ample tush swayed, as if soused, above the sidewalk. She didn't strike me as drunk back in the bar. Not one bit. One tequila shot was too little to provoke the weaving walk and sexy but slurry giggles that floated out of her mouth.

That jerk must have drugged her drink, and it caught up with her slight metabolism in a snap. She fell right into my arms and snuggled against my chest, and her vulnerability, the fact that anyone could take advantage of her in this state made me want to spank her until it burned. This was a problem. Sure, it made my job easy if she were semi-conscious. But there was no way I could fulfill the growing hunger that her proximity stirred, and it did not help matters one bit when she nestled herself in my arms.

She was an escapee, and I was here to seize her and bring her in. Just because she smelled like peach pie was no reason to lose focus.

Do my job and remind myself she had helped her father break into Bunker Inc. and stolen proprietary information.

No matter how tasty her scent, I'd ensure justice would be served, and when she was no longer intoxicated, I'd give the little fool a stern lecture on safety.

*E*yes barely open, I decided to enjoy the ride. I needed more of whatever was in that shot from the Dive Bar, I thought while Thor carried me back to my hotel.

That's right—lifted my full-figured ass off the ground. *The entire way.*

Brutus made me appreciate being treated as if I were light as a feather for the first time ever. In his arms, I had the additional benefit of nearness: I could touch him, plant kisses on his jaw. And it just seemed *right*, you know? His limbs enfolded me like branches, transporting me through the streets of Sacramento. People watched us as if they could absorb romance into their pores via osmosis.

"Will it hurt if I rub it?" I raised my hand to his face and asked, then realized his scars no longer startled me. He went rigid beneath me and quit moving. I dropped my hand before touching him. Every feature of his face conveyed the fact that he wanted to do something savage with me.

We had arrived at my temporary lodging. The creature cradled me stiffly against his chest, standing in the lobby, under the glow of the Arts and Crafts style lights. I noticed our reflection in a gilded, oval mirror the size of a door. The difference in our size was so vast that a soft gasp of surprise escaped my mouth. He held my entire body so it draped across his lower arms, my long black hair spilling to his knees, backlit by the elegant ambiance of the leaded glass lamp shades throughout the foyer. His stance was formidable, shut down, no visible wedge to access his heart. Although his posture appeared to be that of a predatory animal, he didn't scare me. I felt safe in his barbarian arms.

"Saaaayyy." I pointed at him. "How d'you know where my place is?"

"Well, little fool, you gave me your key when I asked for it. The name of your hotel and room number are printed right on it. What would you do if my motives were impure?" He bared his teeth with that remark and carried me effortlessly up the wide marble steps to the second floor. My imagination took me to multiple scenes I'd read with princesses being locked up in a tower.

Yet I was in a lovely mood. No wonder people liked drinking so much. The fear that goons were after me vanished; my world was carefree. This giant was my defender. A grouchy, prickly protector but a guardian nonetheless.

"Hey, you never gave me your name," I said.

"Correct. You never told me yours," the creature growled in a friendly enough way. "You tell me yours, I'll tell you mine."

"Mine's Isabella. Most everyone calls me Bella."

"Well, *Isabella*, my name is Liam Whittaker and the answer is no." I had no earthly idea what he was suggesting; it didn't matter so long as he kept talking. The side effect of potent drink was that his gravelly voice with its iron-fisted essence stirred a furnace in my hoo-ha. It required stoking with his warrior wood.

I cracked myself up and burst out laughing.

He glowered at me, until I settled down and asked him, "No, is the answer to what question?"

"No. It won't hurt if you pet my old wounds." Hercules held me far enough away from him to lock his stare on my eyes and hypnotized me so I froze in place with a single look. Weren't prey supposed to flee the beasts in their surroundings?

He stopped at my suite and set me on the patterned carpet. I swayed as if standing at the bow of a boat, only the ocean was nowhere in sight.

He fiddled with the card and opened the apartment. To steady the motion of the waves, I fisted his black t-shirt in both hands. I reached up to stroke his cheek and chin and he picked me up anew and kicked the door shut behind him.

I took him up on his petting offer. "Oh wow, it's smooth and stiff at the same time. The patterns are as if you have continents outlined on your skin. Although, this side's so clear." I poked his nose reaching for the side without defects, stroked his stubble underneath my palm and giggled. "Such dichotomy between the two sides." Funny, I was growing used to his scars. They didn't startle me as they did back in the Dive Bar. I traced the generous shape of his lip, rubbed the pad of my index finger over the bottom lip, returned to sketch the swirls of his facial markings, back to his lower lip again, and he snapped his teeth down on my finger.

Not so it hurt. But I was caught there, between his jaws. And I couldn't breath. The world came to a halt. There were so many things I should be afraid of with this man, so many reasons if I weren't drunk a million times over. But this one gesture of his snapped me into sobriety and frightened me more than his strange features or presence in my hotel. I couldn't think.

"You're lucky you're drunk," he grumbled.

He let me go and slid me to the ground. The sensation of my body skittering over his was slow and stimulating. I had to bend my neck backward to see him. He wrapped his massive biceps around me when I started swaying and I pretended the moment where time stopped didn't happen. "Boy, I feel great. Do they have any tequila in the mini bar?" I teetered to the bed and fell backward onto the mattress. "Can you help me take off my clothes? I need a hand. Getting undressed is hard."

"Mercy," he said in his rough voice and flung his jacket into the wing backed chair in the corner.

I held my feet up to him, expressing he should remove my shoes. He hesitated and then frowned down at my feet, his hands looked ginormous untying my laces.

"I mean it, I could go for another drink. This is the best I've felt in years. Years. You wouldn't believe how long it's been since there was a real live man in my bedroom. In fact, I don't think I've ever had a *real* man in my bedroom." I cut my eyes up to his angel and demon face, "Hey. What *are* you doing here, anyway?"

"You invited me." He peeled my stinky socks off. "You keep forgetting that?"

So what if he got a whiff of my sweatiness? "Oh yeah, now I do. Gotta question for ya. Can you help me take a shower? The rug moves when I walk."

"Maybe you've had enough. You're lucky I don't take advantage and do all the things I'm thinking about right now."

"Come on. I wanna do shots and be your naughty girl." I waved in his general direction, similar to the Mermaid waving her limbs in the tank. "What are you thinking about right now?"

"I want to pin your hands above your head on that

mattress and bite you hard on the neck. HARD. Luckily, you won't remember anything I'm saying in the morning."

Everything was under water. "Do it! Pick me up like a Viking again, throw me on the bed and take me."

"I don't have sex with drunk girls. Personal rule of mine." His jaw tightened.

"Gah. You're no fun." I sat up, wrestling out of my shirt. "And now? Does this change your mind?" I unsnapped my bra in the front, flinging it in the air. "These are two excellent reasons to revise your personal policy." I lifted a boob in each hand, bounced them for good measure, and put a toe on the floor to keep the place from tilt-a-whirling around me.

"Those are two very compelling reasons that you need protection and have *no business* allowing strange men in your room." He was stroking his own throat, just below the carved out tributaries on his flesh. My insides crumpled a little again at his reprimand.

"*Now*, you're going to do as you're told, be a good girl, and have another shot."

"Yes! Goodie!!!" I threw my arms in the air, fell back on the pillows and watched his first class ass walk to the minibar and pour the entire contents of an airplane-sized bottle of booze over ice.

He returned with a dark look on his face to where I rested and said, "Bottom's up."

That's how I passed out. Nose smashed on the pillow, bottom up in the air, a head full of dreams in which I cleared my father's name and brought him home safe.

BELLA

The dawn cracked my eyes open like raw eggs tossed on cement, and I wondered how a shot or two of tequila turned into twenty. "Oh, my head." I rubbed my temples and squeezed my eyelids shut against the brutal glare. Seated next to me, Gigantor gripped the steering wheel and watched the horizon as if kidnapping drunk girls was an everyday occurrence. "What did you do to me? Where are we?" No answer. "You can't take me somewhere against my will! I have to turn back to Sacramento and my car!"

"How about one question at a time there, Cap'n Tipsy?"

Outside the window, the landscape blurred by, gold-colored dry grass of summer and the dull green of scrub brush. I fell right into this goon's trap. God, I sucked at being on the run. "Dammit," I stomped my Uggs on the floor of his truck.

"What was that again?" He actually glared at me from across the truck cab.

"What? Dammit? I can say dammit as much as I want. *Dammit. Dammit Dammit.*" It felt better to stomp one foot every time I said it. "You're kidnapping me and keeping me from doing what I need to do!"

"Watch your mouth, missy." He grabbed the wheel so tight his knuckles were white during which time I wondered why his icy air of command made me feel hot and wriggly.

And that stupid, sexy voice of his. "We're headed east, passing through the lovely countryside of Nevada, on our way to Maryland. Bunker Inc. headquarters. Put your feet up, relax. Enjoy the tumbleweed."

Just my luck, this dude was a deranged psycho, kidnapping me, and planning to take me to some excluded part of the desert to do me in on behalf of the terrible men who were after my papa. They must think I held the map to his whereabouts. "Where's my stuff?" My stomach plummeted. My laptop was in my suitcase and I had work to do.

"Your things are in the back." He wasn't upset by my state of mind and displayed this by placing an elbow on the windowsill. "Have some of this, you'll feel better." He passed me a to-go mug of coffee. What if I threw it at him and he was forced to stop? Nah. He might crash.

"The sooner you give in, the faster you can help my employer find your father and he'll make amends for what he did."

My stimulating thoughts about the brute fled at his cold, detached accusation. My father was innocent!

"Things will go a lot easier for you if you come along peacefully." His voice was sharp as a scalpel.

"That's the thing. I don't know where he is and even if I did, I would *never* tell you!" This time the heat surging through my body had nothing to do with desire.

I never gave up. Not when they accused my papa of a crime he didn't commit. And not when fucking cancer took Mom too soon, leaving me ten-years-old and trying to help my depressed dad by cooking his favorite tuna casserole each Wednesday.

Like she did.

My papa was sad. He hardly noticed.

No matter how tired chemo made her, she trained me in the care and feeding of Dad. Determined to do a proper job, I kept notebooks full of Mama's direction on how to ensure he didn't miss her too much when she died. The handwritten instructions I jotted down appeared in my memory:

- A sprinkle of cinnamon in his coffee every morning
- The secret to tuna casserole is a half a cup of mayo with sprinkled, crushed potato chips on top
- Use natural cleaner prepared with baking soda, vinegar, and lemon juice to clean the bathrooms and the kitchen

All the note taking and domestic trickery in the world didn't atone for her absence. My mama did her best to fill her void with all the extraordinary things she used to do for our family by teaching them to me. But all it did was cause us to notice she wasn't there. I'd set that special casserole on the table, and Papa and I would lose our appetite.

The cave dweller snapped me out of my daydreaming. "We're pulling in here for gas and food." With that, he parked the truck, and before I knew it said, "Get over here and hold still." He pinned my wrists behind me, palms up, and snapped a pair of metal cuffs on me.

"Are you serious?" My eyes bulged at him.

"As a heart attack." I wanted to smack the snarky smirk off his face. Every minute he detained me delayed my work towards proving my papa's innocence. To think this Creaton made me have sexy feels last night—difficult to believe now.

The long, incessant dry spell my body endured forced her to betray me. Any burly male would do. Oh God, hopefully nothing happened that I'd regret, "Hey, uh. In the hotel room? I was pretty gone. You and I, we didn't... did we?"

He spread his feet to hip width and epitomized the word formidable. "Don't fret." He spoke with eyes crinkled, and lit with an inner twinkle of mischief that almost cracked his stone-faced countenance, which was set in perpetual scowl since we met. "Your virtue is still intact."

This part of him was far more dangerous than the tough guy exterior. This was a male that would be hard to resist, as evidenced by the intense craving crawling over my skin like melted chocolate. This signal told me that the time to plot my escape was now, before it was too late and my biological clock made her alliances clear.

"The handcuffs are necessary when we're going somewhere you might make a run for it. Not gonna happen on my watch, princess."

I briefly clenched my hands and leveled a cold glare at him, "Quit calling me that. I'm nobody's princess."

He arched a confident brow and gave my shape a bold, sweeping gaze which flamed across my curves.

"Sorry." I tried the flies with honey tactic. Catch him off guard. "I understand. You're merely doing your duty."

His harsh response let me know I wasn't deceiving anyone. "Why are you so cheerful suddenly? I'm still taking you in, and your fake obedient act isn't fooling anybody." He doubled his arms across his doorway-sized chest.

His grumpy attitude was reassuring, and I recognized it as a disguise for hidden feelings beneath the rough surface. He wouldn't allow himself to grin at me or show warmth for fear of appearing weak. I should be afraid; instead, his gruff demeanor was somehow reassuring. At least it was honest. It was weird that I could see through this creature's facade, as if I were suddenly a wildlife psychologist.

I needed to date more.

Perhaps I could convince him my compliant put-on was for real. "No one's taken me on a cross-country road trip before. May as well enjoy it!"

Mom's echo from the past spoke inside my brain. A bit of a hippy, she used to advise me: "Savor each day, Bella. There's something to appreciate in every moment." She said the words often enough so they stuck.

Thanks, Mom.

There was indeed pleasure to be found in this occasion, taking a trip across the U.S. with this surly, sinewy creature driving me to parts unknown. I'd have sufficient time to plot an escape plan crossing through states between here and our destination, and once free from the thug, make it safe for my dad to come back. We pulled into the parking area, pinned down at the two short sides of the concrete rectangular lot by either end of a huge neon arch boasting "Nevada 50, Loneliest Highway". On the inside, the truck stop cafe looked the same as a million places in America. Dickies wearing dudes and their baseball cap sporting companions populated the diner and had enormous plates of breakfast in front of them.

I was ravenous. And the brute had his hand at my lower back, guiding me. "Hey. Is that appropriate behavior for transporting a prisoner?" I asked. "I don't *think* so."

"If you prefer, I'll use a waist chain with the handcuffs," he threatened. "That will secure you so I don't need to maintain contact."

Swear to God he enjoyed tormenting me.

The restaurant was old as dirt with black Naugahyde, deep tufted booths. Liam demanded a place in the corner and sat so close his thigh burned mine while we shared a menu.

"Don't get any ideas; this isn't a date," he said.

"If so it'd be the worst date I've ever had." It was a total lie. Even handcuffed, I thought of some way worse dating doozies. Like the dinner with a guy studying mortuary science. He asked if I'd consider a cold bath before sex, and then lay very still. He went to the restroom and I dashed outside as fast as I could. Otherwise, I'd never met a man who intrigued me. I went to school with *boys*. No wonder I hadn't been keen on the dating scene since then.

"So what are you going to have? You must be hungry. Those gummy bears from the mini bar last night wouldn't fill up an ant."

I sat on his "normal side" which sounded wrong as soon as I thought it; they were scars not a rap sheet. I pretended to look at the colorful banners touting professional baseball team mascots. Looks stunning enough to stop traffic were his by birthright. Then the demolition on the other side happened. Wonder how he dealt with that. "I could eat a horse. I'll have the Big Rigger and a chocolate milkshake."

He grinned widely at me for the first time and I felt light-headed. "On one condition. I get a sip of your shake."

I swung my legs below the table. "Answer me this, how am I supposed to eat my breakfast with my hands behind my back?"

"You won't have to feed yourself. I'll do it for you." He sat back on the bench seat and crossed his log-sized arms across his chiseled chest making me worry his sleeves might split.

Our meal came, and ole huge-hands cut my food. The fork and knife looked incompatible with his fingers, which dwarfed the utensils. "That's unnecessary. I promise to sit here and be a good girl and not try to escape."

He halted his sawing at my French toast and jerked his face towards me. The contrast between his breathtakingly handsome and startling, scarred side jarred me. I forced myself not to look away or suck in my breath, wondering why the sudden shift in his behavior.

"You'll. Be. A what?" his deep voice demanded.

I cleared my throat, "A good girl?" I opened my mouth indicating it was time for him to deliver to my tongue another piece of syrup-soaked toast.

He dropped his forehead into his right palm and made a low, guttural complaint, "This *can't* be happening."

"What's wrong?" Leaning towards him, I realized that this annoying giant held my life in his hands. Hands that kept the keys to my shackles safe, and it wouldn't do for him to be impaired by whatever he found upsetting.

"Do me a favor. Finish your goddamn breakfast and quit saying things that force me to wonder about the color of your panties." Liam picked up his cup of coffee and took a loud slurp.

"Oh, so *you* can say dammit but I can't? Mighty chauvinistic of you, Tex." Not to be outdone, I bent my head to my coffee cup and took a loud suck.

Only louder. *Sluuuuuuuuurp.*

The two truckers sitting at the table next to us started cracking up.

Plenty pathetic was the fact that the closest thing to a proper occasion to go out with an alpha male, since ever, was with this husky barbarian who gulped his coffee. A guy hired to seize me and haul my ass in. My excitement over the simple act of sitting next to this Titan was a sure sign I needed to get out from behind a computer screen way more often. No chat room conveyed the same physical thrill as being in Liam's immediate vicinity. The sheer bulk of him and hard, muscled body of a warrior was best appreciated in the flesh.

He shoveled one mouthful at me after the next of syrupy goodness, sausage spice, and interspersed it with sips of my shake. A set of emerald eyes stayed locked on my mouth with every bite or sip I took. I noticed that he moved his thigh away from mine on the bench so we were no longer touching.

My opponent had just revealed his vulnerability. I didn't have any arrows handy, but one thing was certain: this hired soldier had an Achilles heel.

His weakness was me, and I intended to exploit it to the maximum extent.

"$\mathcal{I}$ have to go potty," she said.

"That can be worked out." I didn't appreciate the way her plea made my throat ache a little. Or how I had to steady my right hand carefully while feeding French Toast to her swollen lips.

She was clever as the devil and twice as alluring; I learned that from her dossier: homeschooled herself to take care of her mom during stage four cancer, early admission to the Cyber Security program with Global Knowledge. Not to mention her smarts combined with the lines of her curves, which burned themselves into my brain so I thought of nothing else.

They hired me to deliver her to them, but judging by the stiffness protesting in my pants, I was far from immune to her charms. I wouldn't blame Bella for seeking to capitalize on that. Hell, I would do it if in her shoes. So it landed on me to make sure our relationship stayed professional. Nothing personal, strictly business.

Just a job. Like a hundred others. The money from this project paid enough to get out of the cat-and-mouse game. I trained for this mission my entire career. One worthy of being my last.

I escorted her down the long, wood paneled hallway hung with framed black and white pictures of truck stops from the 1950s and 60s. Bella went ahead of me to the restrooms, and from the back, could admire her jiggling end zone. *Focus. Just get her to Maryland. That's all you need to do. Stop admiring her body parts, for fuck's sake. Besides, girls with looks as pretty as hers are born with a boyfriend.*

After checking that the bathroom was window-free, I undid Bella's cuffs and snapped them on again so that her hands were in front, allowing her to take care of business. I held onto the cuffs preventing her from leaving me and warned, "Hey, so note to self?"

She stared up at me like I was the abominable snowman about to eat her puppy. "Girls need to keep their eyes on their drinks every single minute when they're in a bar. That scrawny dude drugged your drink last night. You're lucky I came along when I did."

"Lucky! If this is luck I never wanna see what you call 'misfortune.'"

"Is that so?" I raised a brow at her. "Don't tarry doing your business in there. I *will* come in after you if necessary."

"It takes trust to build a relationship, you know." She jerked her wrists to the end of her cuff chains three times. "This thing between us won't go anywhere if you can't trust me. Be right back." She pulled the door open and went inside, and out came an older woman with a tight perm and rhinestone encrusted horn rims pulled her glasses down and stared at Bella's shackles.

"We're just trying to spice up our sex life," Bella held up the cuffs and sassed at the woman's obvious distaste. When the duly offended shoved her shiny pink leopard skin print purse up to her elbow and pushed past me, Bella hollered after her, "You can get help with that shitty sense of style, but being a bitch, that's permanent!"

For the first time since I remembered, I tossed my head back and laughed out loud.

With gritty eyes, the headlights coming straight at me for the last two hours weren't making it any better. We'd be at the location I'd plotted for a stopover within the hour.

There were weird caveats required by the men who hired me. Transport the fugitive via Highway 50 from Sacramento to Maryland. No plane trips. They said Bella was clever enough to escape anywhere with plenty of people and exit strategies available to her, making her sound like a seasoned criminal. Fine by me. More transport time meant more hours billed.

I was plenty used to dealing with eccentric employers in my line of work. Besides the trip had been more entertaining than I expected thus far and rather than a criminal mastermind, Bella came off more like an innocent girl in need of safekeeping. She napped earlier, recovering from her roofie hangover, and her gentle snores filled her side of the cab. Now, post-nap, she chatted like a freaking magpie.

"Whatever your boss told you, they lied." She turned the radio on and fiddled with the dial, flipping from one station to the next without landing on a single station.

I slumped in my seat and snapped, "Yeah, okay. Thanks for the intel."

"They framed my dad when he discovered that your employers were the ones behind the theft of client information. They didn't figure anyone would track their hacks but they were wrong. They're only after him now because he discovered their dirty secrets."

"Sugar. I've stood shoulder to shoulder with enough thieves to know one thing: crooks *always* lie. Besides, humans are *never* what they appear, and good people some-times do bad things."

"Meaning?" She tried to cross her arms in a huff, but the cuffs prevented it.

"Meaning, you may look like a rose, you may smell like a rose, but fact is fact. Your dad took money from my client. A shit ton of money. And stealing is wrong, no matter how evil the guy is you're robbing. Just as the old adage says, two wrongs don't make a right." I could feel my temperature rise. "Let me tell you something, you *will* help me make it right."

That kept her quiet for a solid hour. I saw her thoughts spinning like cartoon watch gears over her head as we continued towards Utah, our first stop-over during this road trip.

<hr>

She propped her chin on both fists and asked me out of the blue, "Okay, so if you don't want to discuss the elephant in the room, how about a game of dirty thirty?"

"Wait a minute. What elephant in the room?"

"The elephant: my father's *innocence*."

I pretended not to hear her. Nor did I want to listen to her wax on about the dirty thirty.

Thank you, but no.

"Okay then. Dirty thirty it is. Me and my best friend memorized these conversation prompts from a magazine to whip out any time a date isn't going anywhere. First chal-lenge: when's the best time to have sex?"

I remembered the sight of her jeans as she walked ahead of me towards the bath rooms in the truck stop, "Anytime," I said.

"Hysterical."

Even though I wasn't looking at her I could tell she was rolling her eyes. *Brat.*

"Come on, it's no fun unless you answer honestly. It's the only way we'll learn about each other."

"Bella, you're with a strange man in a strange place, headed to meet the people who initiated this manhunt," I lectured. "Sexy talk is too risky right now."

Unless she wanted to take advantage of the fact that I was a hot-blooded male, in which case her game was right on point. My dick was all ears. But Jesus, I cuffed her, for fuck's sake. If I weren't a decent guy, she'd be putting herself in *real* danger. And the thought of her being careless with her safety made me grind my teeth and breathe through my nostrils.

The little fool.

Unperturbed, she kept going without a care in the world, as if we discussed the weather, instead of her next question. "What are the top five things you search for in porn?"

No mistake, that last question made me madder than a hornet. Only because I thought about the repercussions of saying something like that to a complete stranger. In this case, I was that stranger, and she was lucky, very lucky, that I was not a man to make a woman do something sexual against her will.

I wasn't anyone's hero, and her teasing pulled at me with silken tentacles. I could feel the beat of my heart in my chest, and the hair on my arms stood up as if with static electricity when I propped my left elbow on the steering wheel and faced her straight on to say, "Let's see... my favorite porn always features a naughty brat who can't behave." I slowed my words down for emphasis. "Her Dom grabs her and holds her down on his lap for being a bad girl and he punishes her with a good, hard spanking that reddens herbig, juicy ass while she struggles. Further punishment results in a deep-throated blow job where the brat is forced to take him all the way in her mouth, and finally her Dom fucks her hard enough to break the bed." I glanced at the road and turned back to her again. "How about you? What kind of porn do you prefer?"

The corners of my mouth turned up to see her hands clench and release in their cuffs and her eyes became shiny. It was a relief to have her shut up. I didn't need her to behave with me as if we were as simple as boy meets girl. For one thing, it made my dick hard, and secondly, I needed to remember that Bella's motives were strictly ulterior.

Bella weakly lifted her hands and pointed one finger out the windshield. "Eyes on the road, please."

We traveled all the way to River Song Cabin, an Airbnb I booked for the night. The $64,000 question in my mind? How was I going to make it through the night in close quarters with her wanton innocence without punishing that sassy bottom of hers?

I never met a girl in more need of my discipline.

LIAM

ugitive Recovery Agents' Legal Limits: a protective search should be conducted by an agent of the *same sex* as the prisoner.

We rode in silence the rest of the way to the cabin; my honest and graphic answer to her second dirty thirty question was enough to quash her cheeky bravado. Good. That'd teach her to play with fire.

I pulled into the driveway off the main road through a flat expanse of land, sparsely populated with pine trees, the ground beneath it as barren of vegetation as the air was with our conversation. The parking lot was across the bridge from the cabin, and the footpath over the bridge led to the front steps of the log house. Bella stomped her feet the entire way there. I set down our bags, flexed my fingers, and entered the code to open the keyless door lock.

I heard her boots stepping away from me at a sprint across the gravel behind me, and spun around to chase after her. She slammed to a halt in front of me when a pack of coyotes began screaming from behind the shadowed tree line. These weren't howls, they were high pitched warnings that shot up the spine and shoved down the belly. I grabbed her around the waist and carried her back under one arm.

"Put me down, you oaf!"

Hauling Bella inside, I dropped her on a chair, then tossed our luggage on the living room floor and secured the door. I spun at her and folded my arms across my chest, a feeble attempt at restraining my urges, "What are we going to do with you, Bella?" A vein throbbed beneath the tightened skin on the left side of my face, and I attempted to rub it into submission.

She was frozen in front of me, helpless because of her cuffs. I'd be lying if I said the thought of her at my mercy didn't give me an erection. And yet, it wasn't my place to show mercy in the least. She was asking for it, and I was clearly the right person to make sure she got what she deserved: a good walloping. This girl needed some sense spanked into her if I ever met one.

That was the last semi-rational thought that crossed my mind before I bent down in a tackle position and hefted her over my right shoulder. The thought of taking her over my knee wouldn't go away, and there was only one way to fix that.

I was going to smack the hell out of her broad back end and teach her all of the lessons she needed to learn. Make it so that when I was no longer around, she'd remember this lesson.

She slapped at my back, her blows hindered by the fact that her wrists were bound together. "What are you doing, you barbarian!? You can't treat a prisoner this way! It's against regulations. I'll have your badge!"

I chuckled and felt her bounce on my shoulder. "What

badge? I don't need no stinking badge. I'm a hired gun. I certify myself."

Flicking on the light inside the master bedroom, I was greeted by more wood. What was it with log cabin decor, every room had walls, floors and ceilings gleaming with the evidence of a lumberjack showing off his hard wood. The bed was big though. It would do for the night, and for the session I was planning in my head for Bella.

After setting her on the ground and removing her handcuffs, she didn't disappoint. She attempted to bolt away from me towards the door. I snatched her from behind, letting her kick in my arms as I carried her to the bed, then threw her on the mattress. Her black hair spilled over her shoulders and my eyes devoured the generous lips which gleamed like crystal, her strong brows arching over her large, wistful eyes. My anger receded.

What was I doing?

Then she sat up on her elbows, glared at me, and popped off, "God! First you high jack me out of nowhere, then you bring me to some lame ass cabin in the boondocks and start acting like Ghengis Khan on his period." If she was scared or remorseful for her father's crimes, and possibly her own involvement, I didn't see it. "Thanks to you," she actually shoved her finger at me, "today was a one star shit parade, and if you don't mind, I'd like to get some sleep! *Alone.*"

That did it. And excuse me; Ghengis Khan didn't even *have* a period.

Fugitive Recovery Agents' Standards on Treatment of Prisoners: a strip search should *not* be permitted without reasonable suspicion that the prisoner is guilty of a crime involving drugs or violence.

"*Strip*," I ordered.

Bella went rigid and her eyes bulged.

"*Now.*"

Her voice was shaky and halting when she said, "You can't do this. I'm under your custody—you can't sexually assault me."

"No one said anything about having sex with you. This is about payment for your crimes." I was fully aware that I was on the verge of committing the same acts I was worried about Bella putting herself in danger of with her stupid Dirty Thirty tactics. I was no better than the same common lecher I was trying to protect her from.

The only difference was, I could control myself.

It was to my utter amazement that she pulled her knees under her, stared steady into my eyes and shucked her T-shirt off. Topping those amazingly thick and scandalous thighs and pillowy abdomen were a pair of breasts that taunted me. My hands itched to pull her camisole down and discover the hidden treasure beneath.

This wasn't about that. She needed to familiarize herself with the kinds of consequences she'd face for sassing and disobeying me.

"Off with the pants, Bella. Put your feet on the ground and lay face down on the mattress."

She tipped her head to one side. "But, but you said you weren't going to assault me. Nothing sexual."

"Accurate." I clamped my hands around her ankles and yanked her to the edge of the bed. These things the fairer sex called "leggings" made my job easy. One tug and the stretchy fabric came right off.

Shit. She wore red panties.

My movements were faster than she could anticipate, and

although she struggled, my left knee was at the center of her back faster than she could say, "What in the Sam Hill are you doing?!"

"Patience, Bella. Before you find out, I need you to tell me: why are you being punished?"

"Punished?! What are you talking about, you misogynistic brute?"

"I'll give you one more chance to take this seriously." I was torn between roughing her ample cheeks and diving between them to lap thirstily at her pussy.

Concentrate. Control.

"Remember to look both ways before you go fuck yourself, Whittaker!"

"Have it your way. We'll do ten for tempting a strange man, namely me, and putting yourself in danger," I cracked my open palm down on her fine ass and enjoyed her jiggling flesh. She howled aloud and covered her mouth with her hand, nails painted a sweet pink that contrasted with her nasty attitude.

"That's right, you keep your hands out of the way, little girl." I delivered the next nine at hard, high speed and enjoyed the sight of her trying to scrabble up the mattress, away from the impact. Not a chance.

After ten blows, I knew there was no way I had made a corrective impact on her behavior.

My inkling was verified when she taunted, "Didn't hurt. You can't make me do anything!"

Her defiance stoked my fire and I felt the control I struggled to maintain slipping through my hands. "Excuse me?" I roared at her. It was necessary to clear my mind and take two minutes to breathe deeply and restrain my impulsiveness. There are two emotions that can blind a man: lust and rage. Those were the instincts I currently fought on my own inner battlefield.

Administering discipline in anger was unacceptable. Her carelessness exasperated me, certainly, and this here was for her own good. The only way she'd learn to stay safe. But I needed to calm myself before connecting with her succulent flesh again.

"This time, count aloud for me." I pulled the red panties down to reveal her cherry striped buttocks. "Almost red enough. Think about how foolish it was to bait a guy like me." Before continuing, I gently pulled her panties back up and noted the blotchy flush painting her back which rose and fell in an accelerated pace along with her breathing. "Ten more."

When the next blow landed, Bella began to pound the mattress as if striking the chest of a ravishing male carrying her off to his cave. It had absolutely no effect on my sympathy. Not a bit. "What did I say? You'll count for me, or I'll double your penalty."

"Eleven! I'm sorry. Please don't double my punishment. *Please, Liam.*" A sharp gasp escaped her lips as the sensations of my spankings built.

She was learning. The final nine I burned onto her bottom, enjoying the sweet sound of her pleas and promises to obey while her legs fluttered at the knees in response to my painful correction. I didn't go easy on her and realized my own sexual frustration and aggravation over Bella's reckless behavior: teasing a strange man and trying to booby trap deadly ones drove the strength behind my swats. When I finished, I massaged the kiss-colored, silk material covering her flesh, once again admiring my handiwork.

Bell's entire cheeks were now flushed, and the sight went straight to my cock.

It crossed my mind that I was too hard on her. She wasn't used to someone like me—a veteran of war turned hired gun probably had no business with a woman like Bella: smart, funny, sexy. *Innocent*. Too inexperienced to fear the underlying danger she toyed with. She was a young woman who deserved a whole man, not a course operative with half his face missing, more used to dealing in the currency of criminals than with an ordinary, no extraordinary, girl like Bella.

"No mercy!" I heard the battle cry ring in my ears, snapping me out of my sympathy. If Bella insisted on going against me again, I would have no choice but to treat her without mercy.

At least she wasn't overtly turned on by spankings, as indicated by her struggle.

It would be near impossible to resist her if she was excited by them.

Thank God for small favors.

Or so I told myself.

Until later at bedtime when Bella flipped the table that small favor was sitting on.

Right. The fuck. Over.

BELLA

God he was a hard man. The kind I had avoided all my life. The only encounters with males like him had been in school, which I escaped as soon as possible by finishing early.

He was a bad boy. Going nowhere. The kind who pulled my pigtails in elementary school and called me "brainiac" in high school, as if intelligence were an insult. I'd stopped raising my hand in class by the end of sophomore year and signed up for dual enrollment online that summer, working tirelessly to complete my G.E.D. requirements.

Graduating early meant I had extra time, which would have been wasted in class with kids like this here ogre in my bed. Instead, I researched cyber security certification programs, and convinced my dad to let me sign up for early acceptance with Global Knowledge if they'd have me.

Of course they did. Apple didn't fall far from the tree, and the last name Tate went with ethical hacking like white on rice, best in the business. In a profession where distrust was the premise of the relationship, my papa opened doors for me that would have otherwise slammed in my face. As an inexperienced connoisseur of network infrastructure, I had access to some of the most prestigious penetration tester platforms. Breaking into an organization's security firewall was addictive. And eventually helped me save my father's life when I was able to warn him that Bunker Inc. was penetrating those security vulnerabilities right along with me, only their reasons for doing so weren't ethical.

"Hey, can you please get me my laptop? I need to check out a couple of things."

Liam blinked rapidly and then stared at me. "Ha! Good one."

"Listen, I tried to tell you earlier; you're working for the wrong side. You don't strike me as a bad guy, other than your Neanderthal methods of dealing with women. Confused maybe. After all this is the 21st century and last time I checked there weren't any caves you could carry me off to."

I watched his admirable backside as he yanked open his duffle bag and took out a shaving kit. I know he had just spanked me and observed my naked hiney, and I was doing my damndest to pretend it never happened, or that it turned me on. But the act of him brushing his teeth in the next room struck me as overly intimate. Not once in my entire life had I chatted with a guy while he brushed his teeth.

Other than my papa.

"Anyway," I continued, "these are very bad dudes you are working for; trust me, I know. They framed my father and they're not above putting a bullet through your head if it suits their fancy. Well, I'm sure they'll have someone else do it for them. Can't get their corporate hands dirty."

He was gargling now, not paying the slightest bit of attention and I squinted my eyes at his back while he put toothpaste and brush away and zipped it up into a tidy leather kit.

I grit my teeth and said, "Look. You have to understand one thing about what I did." He walked through the door and his body crowded its frame. "A desperate human becomes an animal. Capable of anything. My paw was caught in a trap, and I gnawed it off to get my father the help he needed. The people who framed my father didn't care one iota about playing fair. Why should I?"

I bit my lip and felt my mouth go dry as I started pacing the wood floor. "In my shoes you would have don't the same thing. Crashing their server was the only choice I had so they couldn't steal from any more accounts. To distract them from finding my father until he was able to flee the country."

"Stop talking." He was pacing the wood floor and coyotes began to yip somewhere in the distance.

I pulled the covers around me so the coyotes wouldn't mistake me for a snack through the window. "Excuse me?"

"You heard right, not one more word about how innocent you and your pops are. You can work all of that out with my employer when I turn you over. Not. My. Problem."

"What do you think is going to happen? You think they're going to slap us on the wrist and let us go? Be real—my father will eventually figure out what it takes to bring them down. People have disappeared from the planet for less!"

His body went suddenly still and a black curtain of contempt fell over his eyes. I decided to leave it alone, sensing that the beast was at his limit. I still had time to think and plan before we arrived in Maryland, which is where this lout was taking me. Corporate headquarters. There they could put the screws on me and try to get to my papa.

Fat chance.

Not even I, computer system spy, knew where he was. But that didn't mean I was giving up. Every good cyber security specialist knew that to effectively penetrate an enemy's system, you had to pivot and approach the problem from multiple sides.

I received the highest score in history from the Advanced Penetration Testing Program.

If I knew one thing it was this: dude was going *down*.

*L*ying on my back next to Brutus Maximus, I smelled the scent of pink grapefruit, which seemed as out of place as a lake trout playing Balderdash. I told myself to listen to the sound of crickets singing outside. Soothing. Peaceful. Sleep-inducing. But that scent filled my nostrils. It had to be rising off of his skin, and it had my mind galloping.

There was no way I could sleep right now.

It was all wrong to have naughty thoughts about a guy hired to deliver me to the hands of my enemy, but I couldn't stop thinking about his hand on my ass.

Spanking me.

Good Lord.

Flaying my emotions apart with his huge hand. Delivering me from worry, and sparking something to life down there.

Apparently the pleasure palace between my thighs refused to let the memory of his improperly firm hand go. I rubbed my thighs together to relieve the pressure and heard his low-pitched voice next to me. "Stop wiggling."

So bossy. I *hated* being told what to do.

That was when the first pivot came to me.

Pleading didn't work. This beast clearly didn't feel pity so it was no use trying to tell him my father and I were innocent.

It was time to fight fire with fire and show no mercy on him.

Every animal, just like every computer system, had its Achilles heel, and I had discovered his. *Too easy.* "Dirty Thirty. Question number three." I heard his quick intake of breath in the semi-dark, and my chest felt like it was floating to the ceiling. I succeeded in a direct hit at the chink in his armor.

Victory was mine. "What's something I could whisper in your ear to get you hard in seconds?"

But the bastard parried at my attack and advanced at me instead when he replied, "How about you call me 'daddy'?"

Whoosh!

Heat flooded the spot I was trying to wipe out between my legs with a rush of sensation.

Daddy.

Definition: the boss in charge. My defender. Definitely not my papa, my *daddy*.

Only he wasn't.

I thought I was shooting an arrow at the gap in his force field, and apparently he had found mine.

It was the very weakness that made me reach over in the dim light of the moon, and trace the jutting curve of his stubborn, sensual lip with my finger.

Which he then sucked.

Oh, the temperature of that mouth. Like fire. I imagined it exploring other hidden places of my body.

In the faint glow I watched him turn slowly towards me, his body occupying a good triple the space of mine.

Trust me, diminutive was not how anyone would describe me. I was a big girl, and big girls came with big curves. For that I was grateful. He placed his right hand over the PJ tank top covering my breasts and with unexplainable, drawn out fashion descended to capture my mouth in his.

I couldn't help it. When he licked my lips open, I complied with a gasp.

Liam was a hired gun, and his kissing game was right on target. It surprised me that a man as rough as he had such sensual moves up his size XXL sleeve.

In spite of knowing better than to sleep with the enemy, suddenly the button throbbing between my legs was begging to be pushed.

LIAM

*S*wear to Christ I never fucked a fugitive before, but let's be honest: she was asking for it.

For this very reason, the legal limits for recovery agents existed. "Unless accompanied by a female agent, male officers should not normally transport females in custody." Up to this point, such restrictions hadn't been necessary. No other escapee ever made me think with my dick.

I had to be a rule breaker. Telling myself I was above temptation. A *real* professional.

Until now.

Bella. Her name meant beautiful, and God knows her body fit the description with enough scenery and curves to keep a man occupied for a lifetime. She didn't shove my hand away when I placed it on her mouthwatering tit, and the way she moaned into my mouth encouraged me further.

I would never force myself on a woman and would gladly hurt a man who did.

Bad idea or not, if I took her, it would be with her consent. I rose up over her, able to see the gleaming pools of her pupils shining in the moonlight. Her mouth was open, and the sound of her breath quickened when I shoved her tank top over her head.

The sight of her mounds, way more than a handful, were topped by dark buds and I wanted to turn on the light so my eyes caressed her with lusting, invisible fingers. Instead, I lowered my face to them. A flash of gratitude that my scars were not so visible in this light passed through my mind, and I pulled on the rigid nipple with my mouth, laving at its pebbled tip with my tongue.

Bella writhed beneath me, and her struggle went straight to my cock. It meant that she wanted me, and was striving to wiggle away from, or straight towards her own desire. My next move was intended to seal the deal on her passion and make her want to call me "daddy".

Tonight I'd been her Dom, and now it was time to show her how her big daddy could take care of her. If only for a night. One thing I learned in hell was that any shot at paradise had to be taken. I was going to enjoy the hell out of the honeyed spot between her legs and ensure that she took the temporary trip to heaven with me.

It was torture, but I raised my head off away from her tits and said, "Take off your panties, little girl. Daddy needs to make sure your pussy is ready to be fucked." Her breath hitched at the phrase but there was no protest.

Ours was a stare down that lasted longer than the average couple doing it for the first time. She was my prisoner and I was bringing her in. Quite the complication. My battle mindset taught me to keep myself under control, no matter how chaotic my surroundings. In this case, the pounding desire to be inside Bella was too much and I needed to keep it under wraps. I planned to. But right now, my dick was in charge, and let's be honest, he wasn't always the brainiest guy in the room.

The tension blew out of me when she lowered her hands

to her waist and shimmied out of the red, silk panties. Even in the unsatisfactory light, I could see her puffy lips below. They pleaded for my mouth, but I had to touch them with my fingers first, explore them and discover her private places by stroking them with my hands.

Velvet. Her sweet spot felt like stroking velvet, and I held my palm over its soft secret, claiming it as my prize. I'd learn her treasure by heart so I carried it in my memory even after I took her in.

Bella's breath stilled, until I slid one exploratory palm between her thighs and found them clenched together. "Let me explore you, Bella. We can give this night to each other and go back to what we know has to happen tomorrow. But right now, let me take you to paradise, little girl."

She slid her legs apart beneath me and my fingers glided into the tropical silk between her legs. It was a wonder men got anything done at all when women held such power there. It rendered me stupid, but even in such a state, I could still please her.

If the two greatest warriors were patience and time, like Tolstoy said, then I was the greatest goddamned soldiering son of a bitch.

I began to stroke her slick button, and listened to her breathing quicken. Lowering myself to sip her juices, I was rewarded by her gasp, and the way she flung her arm across her eyes in surrender, shutting out the visual reality to absorb herself in a more sensual and heady place. Bella shivered in anticipation and I felt bigger and stronger than any fighter in the field.

A body like Bella's was worth a lifetime of waiting, and I'd take my time getting her ready for how I planned to make her ride my formidable cock. Not bragging, just stating the facts. Throughout my life I'd had enough experience to know that it took some getting used to because of its size. I slid my massive finger to her sweet, gripping channel, and lowered my face to flick at her tasty clit with my tongue. I drew it into my mouth, gently plunging at her core with two fingers, tracking her climax down before I dared to seek my own.

Patience, time, and my own addition to the mantra: *technique*.

Perfecting pussy is the warrior way.

*A*dmittedly, my sexual encounters have been limited up to this point. Awkward scrabbles on the couch with pimply and retainer-wearing admirers who I met through online gaming platforms. There was the one actual trip to the bedroom where my virginity was taken in a clumsy and rushed attempt at penetration. The second, literally I could have counted to one, "Squirt" (as I nicknamed him) was inside and he hit his Big O, leaving me unsatisfied and ickified at the splooge of wetness between my legs.

At least there were no worries of pregnancy. I took care of that by getting protection. Let's just say, the encounter didn't leave me with high hopes for ecstatic encounters with male counterparts.

How wrong I was.

Granted, Liam was older than me. I had noticed the slight creases at the corners of his eyes which told me he wasn't always such a stern and grumpy Gus and had smiled at some point in his life. He was smiling some of the time.

When he laid his fingers on me down there, I figured that was as good as it got. *Ha! Guess again, Tate.*

This was no awkward waiting while he played with the wrong spot, missing my orgasm entirely. It didn't leave me frustrated and yearning to touch myself, or hoping he would leave so I could play with my toy on myself. Sometimes with guys that was the best way to go, take care of it on your own. Lots less embarrassment involved for everyone.

Not in Liam's case. With his technique; patient, determined, and accurate, all I had to do was lay back and relax. The entire experience was such a relief. That a man could deliver, with two digits and his unhurried confidence, as if his fingers were speaking directly to my clit, "Here I come. Get ready. I *will* find you and make you beg for Daddy." His sharp shooter focus was on point and paid off between the sheets.

Those were my thoughts *before* I felt his tongue on me. His fingers continued to gently piston my pussy, and I saw him go down to join them. I should have known, but I couldn't have known how this boy, this man, my *daddy* was going to use his mouth on me. Nothing in my experience had prepared me for such sinful delights.

He lifted my hips in the air, placing both palms under my buttocks, and my core ached at the sudden absence of his fingers inside of me. I could see the faint tributaries of the scars on the left side of his face and realized they were no longer a shock. Since they were part of *him*. No sooner did that random thought dart across my mind, when all capacity to think vanished with a fractured moan that trailed out of my mouth.

Liam had placed his tongue on me and was using it to swirl erotic circles around my actual clit. Eureka! He abso-fucking-lutely found it. He was making a meal out of it, sucking, caressing and consuming me with his mouth and tongue, while I clawed at the chenille coverlet beneath me. It was a good thing we were in the middle of nowhere, as evidenced by the coyotes suddenly howling as a mirrored reflection of my response to this man's amazing skill.

Those wild beasts knew exactly how I felt.

Liam moved one hand under my tailbone, balancing the weight of me there with no effort, so that he could return his fingers inside of me. It only took a little pumping and encouragement on his part, and the combination of his searing and lashing tongue, along with his probing at some previously unknown, overly sensitive spot inside, made me squeeze from the deepest part of me and explode onto his face. I couldn't help it. I screamed and howled like those coyotes and shoved myself onto his mouth, begging him to give me more.

Which he did.

Stamina. That was different. He was taking care of *me*, and judging from the groans he made from time to time while devouring my pussy, it appeared he was actually enjoying himself.

His next words left no doubt in my mind, "God Bella. You're fucking delicious."

So lucky, no lucky wasn't the word. This man was as fearsome in bed as he was out of it. Even with my limited and disappointing sexual history, I realized this man was a prize. More than that.

This man was a *daddy*. What it would be like to actually have such a man in my life as more than just my warden?

*B*ella came three times in my mouth, and I wanted to savor her flavor for as long as I could. This was quickly becoming a dangerous game and it was clear why the rules for fugitive recovery existed. To avoid complications like those I was feeling. At this point, Bella didn't seem like a complication she felt like a revelation.

Was it my dick doing the thinking? We hadn't even had sex yet, but tasting her pussy was transformational. I wanted to keep going. All night, into the next day, into the next year even.

But we had places to go. I had to take her in. And after that? The odds were stacked against us.

Besides, Bella was talking to me. "Come here." She tugged gently at my hair. I climbed up to her and positioned myself over her delicious titties, letting them scrape my chest while resting on my forearms so I could take her in. Then she did something that completely unmanned me.

She caressed my scars.

My pulse raced and my breath grew ragged as she reached up to trace the tips of her fingers across the burned tissue, and the foundation of my features still discernible beneath the partially dissolved flesh. A jawbone, chin, my nose and brow. Her deliberate tenderness towards the part of me that repulsed most people ignited something inside. Something I long believed to be dead.

It was strange to feel how her smooth, delicate skin traced the furrows and rough trenches of my face. "Does it bother you?" she asked.

She wasn't supposed to care. My client told me this was a woman who ruthlessly destroyed companies and took from others without remorse. What Bella demonstrated didn't line up with that profile.

Bella had shown me she was sensitive, not cold-blooded. I just couldn't see her stealing from others when she had directly shown me the generosity of her spirit.

I answered her. "It doesn't bug me. I like it when you touch me. It used to hurt. A lot. Over time, the skin there has grown less sensitive."

"Is it okay then, me touching you like this?"

"Little girl, you can touch me any damn way you please." The yipping coyotes started up again, emphasizing the beastly and carnal craving I had for Bella.

I could practically hear her thinking in the near dark and wondered what she was up to. "Can I touch you…" she slid her hand from my face to my boxers which were stretched out to their limit by my eager dick. "…here, Daddy?"

"Oh God, yes, Bella." She rubbed the head through the flannel and I stayed frozen above her.

"Can I take these off?" she asked, tugging gently at the band of my shorts.

"Anything. Anything you want. Do it to me."

She took her hand away, stopped touching me. "Will you take me back, Daddy? Will you take me back so I can find my papa and make sure he doesn't get hurt? Please?"

Rolling onto my back, I stared at the moonlit knot patterns in the pine above us. Females were so goddamned complex. If I said the wrong thing, this would all be over. She had me in a trenched-in position, where there was no declaring neutrality. Say yes, lose my shot at early retirement. Say no, say sayonara to the finest pussy I'd ever tasted and the little girl that I wanted to claim as mine.

"Bella, you're putting me in an impossible situation, and I despise being manipulated."

"I think you put us in this position. You're the one that told me to call you 'daddy'. Pretty sure that's not in the bounty hunter's playbook. Is it?"

My kitten's voice had a bite to it, and I had to admit she had a point.

I did start this.

"I'm not a bounty hunter," I growled, "but you're right. I started it, and I'll tell you something else right now." I moved my hands to her breasts and gently twisted her nipples between my fingers. *I'm not done with you yet.*"

There were those berries that you found at the end of summer: picked over by bears, or so nibbled by hornets they'd disintegrate to mush in your fingers when picked. Or berries that clung greedily to the vine, waiting for some hint of rain at the driest end of the season, but withering in place before it came.

In contrast, Bella was a sun-ripened berry in the peak of summer brought to fruition by the generous rains of June. Sweet and yielding to my mouth. Every part of her that I pressed to my lips was juicy, youthfully rounded and begging to be consumed.

I couldn't wait any more to fully possess her fruit.

"Tell me something, precious."

She bucked ever so slightly beneath me in response to my hands on her. It was enough for me to notice. I noticed everything about her, and it didn't escape me that this was exactly like being on the hunt.

Intimate pursuit.

"Do you think you can fit this inside of you?" Still on my

back, I moved my hand down to cup my cock. "More than anything, that's where I want to be right now."

Her breath quickened and she ran her hands over my pecs, trembled her fingers up my neck and stroked my face again. Then slowly downwards, hooking her thumbs in the waistband of my boxers, pulling them out to accommodate my rigid girth, which was distended and swollen to the point of pain, as it had been since meeting her. It shocked her. I could tell by the way her hand flew to her chest and she gasped as if seeing a ghost.

"Touch it for me, precious."

She drug her hand over my abs, and finally landed on my naked cock. Bella rubbed small circles at the head, spreading the pre-cum like anointing oil.

"I want to fuck you like a good girl tonight. Are you going to behave and touch yourself for me?"

"Oh," she said. I had blindsided her.

"Oh what? Are you thinking about disobeying Daddy?"

"No, I don't want another spanking," she said. "I want to be a good girl for you, Daddy." Her words accomplished the impossible. They made me even harder.

I grunted my attempt at restraint; she was better at turning me on than she had a right to be, reminding me I was playing with fire. A fact that was burnt into me when she grasped as much of my shaft as she could in her left hand, and started to finger herself with her right.

The suppressed squeals she made when stroking her clit, turning herself on in front of me, pushed me to the brink of danger. If I weren't careful, I'd blow my load in her hand. Instead, I pulled away to look at her. My eyes had adjusted in the dark and I could see the glimmer of excitement on her slick pussy lips.

"That's it, sweetie. Touch yourself for me. Let Daddy

watch and I'll give you a nice reward." Her technique was clumsy and all the more sweet in its display of innocence and inexperience. I was going to change that by applying everything I could to making her come.

As often and as hard as possible. "Do it faster. Show me how you like to excite yourself," I said.

It was too much, the sight of her sweet little hood being shoved from side to side by Bella's delicate fingers; every now and then, the sassy little button popped out for me to ogle. "I can't wait anymore. I'm going to get on top of you and shove myself inside. I need to be in your pussy, baby."

Her panting and keening were inarticulate as far as words went but they spoke a language I understood. Then she spoke, "Ohhh, please. I want…" I pinched her nipple hard between my fingers, increasing her greed. "I need…"

"What do you need, baby?" I rose up over her again and placed the head of my cock at her drenched entrance. "Is this what you need?"

"Mmmm." It was hard to tell if it was a complaint or plea.

"The more you whine, baby, the more I want to fuck you."

"Yes! I want that. *Please.*"

"If I give it to you, will you do as I say? Are you going to come along with me, no trouble?" I gave her tit an affectionate slap, knowing it would only heighten her sensations and leave her craving more.

Her hair was satin in my hand as I pulled it sideways to expose her neck to my mouth, and nibbled from collarbone to beneath her ear. "Yes, I'll do anything you say. I promise, just please! Take me anyway you want."

"Are you certain? I must be sure I have your consent to put my cock in you. Convince me you want it." Admittedly, I was trying to tease the fuck out of her, make her as horny as she made me feel.

She pursed her lips and actually pouted at me. "Why don't you make me? I'm ready to see if Daddy's dick will fit inside of me or not."

"Hold still, baby girl. You're about to find out."

*M*y screech of surprise was muffled as he slammed his lips onto mine, pinning my wrists down next to the sides of my head. I mewled into his mouth, realizing that I was finally going to get what I'd begged him for.

Raising my head off the pillow to return the kiss, I wiggled uselessly under the strength of his arms that held me in place. No matter how hard I struggled to be free of his hold, my effort was feeble.

He growled over me as I continued to try and twist my wrists free, and I could feel his bulge, just resting there, outside my pussy. He made no attempt to shove inside, and it maddened me, making me increase my efforts to kiss him back forcefully, to tease out his ardor to the point of no control. I *wanted* him to take me.

Suddenly, he broke away from me and I watched as he admired the sight of his cock, poking out from my pussy lips. "Look how good we look together, baby girl. Amazing."

"Let me go, Daddy." I twisted my arms under his fists, and did the same with my hips so that it created a wet-hot friction between us. He made a single piston with his hips, creating the erotic sight of his cock head grinding into my clit. I gasped, "Oh, God," and continued to struggle beneath him.

"Don't you know the harder you try to get away, the more I want to capture you?" His hand held my throat and he bit my lower lip, growling at me. "Do you promise to be a good prisoner and do as I say?"

Great, now the thought of being his captive excited me. I wanted him to force me, to take me however he wanted and make me beg. Let's face it; I wanted to be his sex slave. I didn't recognize the blubbering groan as my own, but it pressed past my lips before I could stop it.

"Are you going to follow my rules from now on, and do as you're told?"

I could only nod my agreement since the sensation of his cock giving my clit a massage from the outside made me mute. All at once, Liam apprehended the base, almost with hostility, and laid siege by slapping it at my oversensitive bud.

"It's 9:32 p.m., Bella," he said out of the blue.

"Uhhhhhhhhh." My moan trailed off to infinity. "Okay," I managed to say. "And?"

"You're to remember this time distinctly so every time that group of numbers appears on your phone or watch, you think of me and how I slapped your pretty clitty."

I couldn't help it. I moaned again. To be honest, I liked the way he commanded me and began to fantasize that I could be his captive for more than just a few days. What if we could continue this for real?

"Spread your legs, Bella. Open up for Daddy so he can fuck you hard. That's what my baby girl needs more than anything. Some good cock to take her mind off things."

I did as I was told and he sat up between my legs, placed

his palms under my thighs, and shoved my legs apart as far as they would go.

"Let's make it so you can't walk tomorrow, shall we?" He lunged forward and pushed himself all the way inside and withdrew at a leisurely pace, repeating the process over and over again until I couldn't formulate a single coherent thought.

I knew it was coming every time, the full force of his hard penis, but the highly responsive reaction of my pussy caught me off guard. Things went black in front of me. I had to shut my eyes and it was as though my mind had been cut free from its chains of worry, regret, and grief. It drifted to the ceiling, past that—to the stars, and meanwhile this terrible, wonderful beast above me continued to fuck me senseless.

"Oh God, you're fucking meeeee..." my voice trailed off.

"Yes. I am." He thrust each syllable for emphasis. "You're pussy is *insane*."

"But you're fucking me...you're fucking me *so* good. Oh. My. God." I grabbed the sides of my head, covering my ears, trying to decrease the overwhelming assault to my senses that Liam was delivering. "I'm gonna, Daddeee, I'm gonna..."

"That's right. I'm right here, all the way inside you. Fucking your tight little pussy." He slammed into me, over and over again —claiming me, making me his. "It's like your sweet cunt is tugging and stroking at my cock. You're going to make me come, baby."

I raised my hands from where they were clawing at the comforter and placed them on his hips, helping him get the leverage he needed, pulling him into me hard. "Is that what you want, sweetie?" Was he taunting me? "Is that what you were waiting for?"

I screamed when he exploded inside of me. The fact that I made him arch his back and thrust his chin to the sky made me claim my fourth orgasm of the night. But who was counting?

Liam collapsed on the mattress at my side and pulled me to him. I could hear his heart beating like a hammer behind his chest wall. And I lay there until the powerful pulse of it subsided. It calmed me.

So did his words as he wrapped me in his arms and pulled me to his chest from behind, "I'll keep you safe, Bella. Go to sleep. I'll be right here next to you."

Laying pressed against him, his hand covered my fist and was three times the size of mine. I fell asleep and dreamt of an imperfect love that conquered corporate goons and battle scars.

That true love, in spite of its flaws, spread security and belonging like a blanket over everything it touched. If only it were real life instead of just a dream.

BELLA

fire·wall

/ˈfī(ə)rˌwôl/

COMPUTING

A part of a computer system or network that is designed to block unauthorized access while permitting outward communication.

I thought it was my pussy that needed the most attention, and Liam certainly attended to her last night. She fell asleep purring after contentedly, licking her paws clean of her five course meal.

What I didn't recognize, and should have, was my urgent need for protection. When was the last time I felt safe? Like everything was okay? When was the last time I didn't have to worry that if I wasn't good, something terrible and untamable was going to make things very bad for our family?

Like cancer.

I don't think I'd had that carefree little kid feeling since long before mama died. The final memory I have of that happy-go-lucky reality was the day, singing on the swing set in our backyard, wondering if Dad was going to take us out for ice-cream after dinner. That was my biggest worry. Would I get ice cream after?

I pinpointed the moment when anxiety abated for the first time since that childhood swing set moment. 9:20 p.m. last night.

Before I woke up from my dreams, instead of ice cream, lollipops and lemon drops, I stared up at a three story sized rendition of the weekly cleaning routine I made for myself after Mama died. At the time I wasn't proud of the fact that I kept a household running at ten years of age. It was out of a sense of desperation that I put my list together. It felt as if I were trying to free climb a marble wall, barehanded, without a helmet, rope or carabineers.

My father came home from work every night, poured himself a scotch, and sat in the recliner he had pulled to her side of the bed, staring at the pillow. Only she wasn't there anymore. We would never hear her singing Loretta Lynn at the top of her voice in the kitchen or see her setting her famous seafood lasagna dish on the table saying "ta-da!".

Never again would my friends and I collapse in giggles as she drove the back roads, making the car "dance" in gentle swerves as she boogied along behind the steering wheel. I tried so hard to be just one tenth of the woman she was for us all and felt I failed miserably.

Worst of all because no matter how hard I tried to do a good job, I failed her. I couldn't save her from dying.

In my dream, the weekly cooking, cleaning and shopping routine unfurled like Royal silk, spilling over the roof of the tall building with bullet points suggesting: clean sink, counters, stove, mop, etc.

There were blank lines to fill in meals of the day. Mama

told me the best way to plan a menu was to do it for the entire week; purchase everything I needed on the same day in the supermarket. That way I would have a plan.

"You are such a smart girl, Isabella. Just remember that a goal without a plan is just a wish." All the planning, all the goal setting, all the intention in the world couldn't bring her back to life.

I graduated early from the Cybersecurity training program at Global Knowledge, the youngest graduate in their history. In spite of my insecurities, it wasn't the challenge of the job that made me struggle. The mostly male colleagues I worked with, older and more seasoned in the business than I, resented the success I had in my first year as an employee in the advanced penetration unit, the most prestigious system vulnerability tracer in the world.

They worked us to the point of exhaustion. A lot of my colleagues struggled to succeed not with the physical work demands, but with the social part. Their innate introversion made it hard for them to communicate with clients since they were more comfortable testing penetration tactics on machines than working with people.

Again I thanked my mama for the ability to get along with almost anyone. Taking over the household operations as a kid meant I learned to communicate with teachers to grocery store workers to bus drivers to gardeners and more. I negotiated with the landscaper a lower price by hiring him to cut our grass twice a month, the butcher in the deli expected me every Tuesday afternoon after school and set aside the tastiest and most economical cuts of meat that he had available that day.

It was scary, and I missed her every day. That practice, play acting I was grown-up, meant I was way better prepared for the job when I actually became one.

The dream of my weekly household routine snapped up

to the rooftop, like a cheap rollup blind that gets tugged and released. It did so as a bearish paw flung itself across my body and pulled my bum towards his very alert and awake cock. The remnant of my dream had my family at the forefront of my mind and I didn't feel so safe and secure as I did when I went to sleep last night in Liam's arms.

I knew that he and I would get to our destination, sooner rather than later, and that time was running out. I swung my legs over the bed and stood up. It was three steps to the shower and I rushed inside to close the door and lock it behind me.

It wasn't a Hollywood shower; I got it over with quickly, and covered my entire person with clothing so as not to remind him of what had transpired the night before. This was going nowhere, no matter how tempting and yummy I found him.

It was time to extrapolate the data required for the completion of my challenges. Those being: identify further vulnerabilities within the company that framed my father, and make it safe for him to return stateside.

If working that plan meant exploiting Liam's vulnerabilities, so be it. I would simply have to ensure that my cunning scheme to save my papa, didn't wake up Liam's daddy side again.

Papa was someone I loved and cherished. *Daddy* was someone I couldn't resist.

But in order to keep my affections protected, I needed to erect a firewall. I had to hold back. Handing Liam any part of my heart was a chance I couldn't take.

If I was going to save my papa, ditching Daddy was top priority.

*S*he was looking at me, I could tell, so I kept my eyes shut in pretense of sleep. I didn't know if I could resist her soft, berry-kissed mouth first thing in the morning. Today would be our longest yet on the road and there was no time to further indulge my cock, even though it woke up thinking its God given right was to dive into some pussy. Specifically, Bella's pussy.

No matter how much I wanted to explore her further, we needed to hit it and quit it. So my arousal conflicted with relief when she hopped up and got into the shower without prompting. She was an early riser like me, the sun outside was barely painting the bottom of the sky orange-pink over the flat topped rocks, and I tried to convince myself I wasn't in the mood for cuddling anyway.

When it was my turn to clean up I locked her up again and was glad to hear her resort to her usual spitfire tactics when I snapped the cuffs on her wrists. "Jeez, don't you think you should be off arresting real criminals somewhere? This is a complete and total waste of time." She was sitting on the bed and slammed both feet on the ground to emphasize: *total, waste, time.*

To the contrary, my time would be better compensated than any other in my career and make me pretty again. I didn't plan on letting her brattitude get in the way of that.

At mid-day, we stopped in El Pueblo and rolled through a drive through. Bella asked sweetly if she could get a McFlurry with M&M'S Candies, and I snapped at her in self defense, "*Whatever.*"

"Okay, how about the ten piece Chicken McNuggets Meal with a McFlurry? And ranch dressing on the side, please."

I was lucky she couldn't read my thoughts, because she would discover that when she was sweet to me like this, I was under her spell. If she'd ask me to leave the cuffs off, I might actually consider it.

"Just don't get it on the seat." The words came out of my mouth as a low guttural sound.

"Sheez, okay. I'm not a little kid you know. I'll keep your precious seats clean." Her lips were pressed into a white slash.

Much better. Her sharp tongue was easier to resist, even if it did make my palm itch to blister her bottom.

We ate in silence, and I kept my eyes strictly on the road, not wanting to see face-front that which I observed out of my periphery view, her dipping and licking ranch dressing off of every single fry.

Terrible temptress. I watched the tree line on the sprawling range lining the highway, and polished off my burger instead of feasting on her the way I wanted.

In my fantasy I pulled into an abandoned rest stop, yanked her to the edge of the passenger seat, insisted that she "Spread 'em," after I ripped her panties off. Diving at that scandalous pussy with my tongue and…

Apparently, she wasn't the type to stay mad for long. "Hey, I was just curious, how old are you?" she asked.

Mentally shaking the image of her splayed half-naked across my truck, thrashing her passion out on the seat, moaning her excitement out into the parking lot behind me. "Forty-three," I said. "Why?"

"Just trying to get to know you is all. We still have a long way to go. Might as well entertain ourselves along the way. Did you know I was twenty-five?"

"So said your dossier. I'm aware."

"So not only did you do the nasty with your prisoner, you totally robbed the cradle. Doesn't that bother you?"

"Does it bother you?"

That shut her up. For a minute.

"Why do you want me to call you daddy?

"Because it's hot." I allowed my eyes to caress her with invisible fingers in a slow once-over.

She put her cream colored sneakers with rainbow colored stripes on the dash, and I found myself not giving a flying fuck whether she got it dirty or not. I'd happily clean up after her to earn the privilege of lapping at those tanned legs with my eyes.

Even if we were on the way to some people who happened to be very pissed off at her right now. She could make her reparations, and we'd move on from there. All she had to do was show them how she gained access to their machines and escalated her privileges for a takeover of their computer systems. I'd be with her the entire time. Protecting her.

Call it a "change of mission description". I'd still do what my client hired me to do, I'd just hang around to ensure the target's safe exit afterwards.

She interrupted my thoughts and said, "Seriously, Liam. I

know it excited me to hear you say it, but how did you land on that nickname?"

Done with her lunch, she began tucking cartons into the to-go bag.

"Obviously I want to fuck the shit out of you," I said. "I think I made that clear. But I also want to take care of the woman I'm with. That's the daddy part. When you call me daddy, it enhances things. Not only am I in charge of pleasing your pussy, but also fighting to protect you and keep you safe."

Bella opened her mouth to speak, and closed it again.

"What? What were you going to say?"

She began to tap her lip. "I was going to say, you've got yourself into a real pickle haven't you?"

"How's that?"

"Well, you made my pussy meow, you "fucked the shit out of me", to use your elegant choice of words, and now it's your actual job to deliver me to some very bad guys who will put the serious hurt on my safety. Your daddy status is in peril because of what you've been *paid* to do. Put me in danger."

"They haven't paid me yet. Not in full." I took a swig of root beer, and picked up her hand next to mine, checking out the small group of calves crowding a water hole in the middle of an isolated field off of the road.

"There's one thing you clearly don't understand about me, precious."

"What?"

"I'm not *in* peril. I *am* the peril."

Drive through food was getting old, so I decided to make an exception for dinner.

After filling the tank, and allowing Bella to use the indoor restroom alone since there was absolutely nowhere she could escape to from this desolate gas station and mini mart, I searched the nearest restaurant between here and the next place I rented for us to stay.

There was a roadside steakhouse up ahead, not five miles from our next stop over. We pulled up outside the place which bragged, "Steaks, Seafood, Chops" in neon and I asked her, "If I let you go, are you going to be good?", holding the key to the hand cuffs up to impart my meaning.

"I promise." She rubbed her wrists dramatically. "Please, just let me be free of these for a bit. Not like there is anywhere to run to from this place. It's surrounded by cow fields."

I arched my brow at her and gave her the once over. "Alright, but I'm watching you."

"You gonna watch me swig a cocktail down like Kool Aid?" She swished past me, through the large wooden door of the restaurant. "Cause being your captive makes me need a drink!"

"You can have *one*. Don't want you getting out of control." I scowled at her. "*Again*."

She turned pink and she spun around to face me. "Spoil sport."

I stopped directly in front of her, and it was impossible to avoid her cherry colored lips. They practically shouted at me. Bella leaned towards me, pleading with her eyes and I noticed her two front teeth sweetly peeking out from below her lip. Even they appeared to implore "Kiss me."

Kiss her, you stubborn fool. Girls like this don't come along every lifetime.

I listened to her silent plea. The soft landing on those plump, beckoning lips was more appetizing than the smell of grilled food in the air. And then, when she made herself biddable, compliant and eager with her mouth, I claimed her.

My prize.

Right there in the foyer of the restaurant, like every soldier battling for territory before me, I fought to show her she was mine. I grabbed her ass and pulled her toward me.

"Ahem," an unwelcome sound, that of a high-pitched throat clearing itself, interrupted our exploration.

Bella turned away from me and I had to talk myself down from yanking her back.

Mine.

I didn't like her out of my reach.

The waitress had a high ponytail and a choker which wrapped around her neck like a silver snake. She seated us and asked, "Will this be on separate checks?"

"Absolutely not," I said and pulled Bella closer on the bench seat next to me.

Bella started humming "Girl from Ipanema" and I asked, "Do you by chance have a cocktail menu?"

"One moment." The sour server spun away.

Bella started crooning and it was clear she was one of those people who didn't let the fact that she couldn't sing to save her life stop her.

"Tall and tanned and young and lovely…" she closed her eyes and swayed, and all of the sudden stopped. I was grateful for the reprieve from her flat as a pancake version of the song. Bella said, "I think our waitress is into you."

Before I could answer, we heard a shriek from the back. Said waitress. Her voice packed a punch coming from someone so diminutive that a slight breeze could have blown her away. "Carlos! How many times do I have to tell you… Hot Food Hot, and Cold Food Cold! I'd explain it again, but I'm out of puppets and crayons!"

Bella's eyes were the size of teacups and the waitress returned to ask, "Did you decide on drinks?" As if she hadn't just pulled the screaming banshee move in the back for us all to hear.

"I'll have a margarita, please. Blended, no salt," Bella said beside me under the protection of my arm.

"For you, sir?" the waitress asked me.

"Iced tea, please. And she needs two shots of Don Julio in her margarita."

The waitress whirled around again and headed for the bar, and Bella said, "If she's not careful, she's gonna wear a hole in the carpet. And if you're not careful," she pointed at me, "I'm gonna ask you to marry me, ordering me *two shots*. And you said I could only have one drink—kidder." She playfully hit my shoulder.

No one ever accused me of being a playful guy, but Bella made me feel light. Carefree. And let's face it, our situation was anything but. I had to take her in. She swore she was innocent. With every mile I was putting behind me on the way to our destination, the voice of doubt spoke a little louder in my ear.

This is why a male recovery agent and a female fugitive didn't make a whole lot of sense. But in this case, I had been more than willing to make an exception. The price was right.

Enough to pay for the reconstructive surgery for my face, the cost of which had been denied by the insurance company because it was cosmetic. They'd rather I walk around looking like a Halloween mask, scaring young children and shocking the hell out of grown ups. Thanks for your service, Sergeant Whittaker, good luck getting through life with half a face.

Hey, at least I was alive.

And when this opportunity presented itself, I jumped at the chance. What person in my shoes wouldn't? If I had a dime for every time a criminal told me they were innocent, I'd be a very rich man by now.

Bella was obviously kidding when she joked with me about marriage, and yet I felt my ribs squeeze tight over the desire to own her for as long as possible. I was jealous at the idea of her seriously wanting to marry anyone *but* me, understanding logically that my envy was a lost cause. I was hired to bring her in. Nothing personal. Just doing my job.

"It's gorgeous!" Bella exclaimed when we pulled up at the limestone cottage next to the lake. Unlike the arid surroundings of the place we stayed last night, this spot smelled of grass and algae.

I carried our bags inside and hid the valuables, in other words the truck and handcuff keys, in the mini safe beside the bed. "Could you go for a swim? Wash off the travel dust?" I asked her.

"That sounds delightful."

Bella ran across the short lawn to the dock in front of our cabin, stripped off her clothes on the way and dove from the pier. The dock was still warm beneath my feet, marked by the sun's kiss from the long, hot day.

I could smell the wet earth below, where the rocky gravel painted its shoreline in shades of gray and white. Gray and white, not black and white.

Nothing was black and white. Especially not this thing between me and Bella. Watching her make clean strokes in the water, her elbow rising above her head, feet paddling as she swam away from me, I thought *either this girl was my dream come true, or she was playing me to get what she wanted. Pretending to be attracted to me in spite of my ugly.*

After our swim, I kissed Bella's cold lips. "Hey, you're cold. What say we take a warm shower."

"Together?"

"That's what I had in mind."

"Because you want to shower with me, or because you want to keep an eye on me?"

"Would it make you mad if I said 'both'?"

"No, I'd rather you be honest. It's not like I can go anywhere though. The keys are in the safe, and you made sure we were staying in the middle of nowhere again."

She noticed, which meant she was paying attention to any opportunity for escape. That's why, after the shower, I felt it best to cuff her. Her mind was whirling so fast; I could practically hear her thinking. I decided it was best not to take a chance freeing her while I was sleeping and vulnerable.

I forgot that with Bella in the room, I was defenseless whether asleep or awake. Exposed to her if she wore cuffs or not. Because she had her words.

"Dirty Thirty." She giggled and pleasure pulsed in my veins.

"Not that again." I groaned. "I thought we agreed not to play this game anymore."

"Hey, it's not my fault you ordered me two shots of Don Julio. Tequila makes me do bad things."

Okay, she had my attention. "Such as?" I moved closer to erase the distance between us.

She looked up at me, nonplussed. "Such as ask you, have you ever had sex with someone wearing handcuffs."

I clenched and released my hands, feeling a little feverish. "Surprisingly not…yet. I'm definitely willing to give it a try." I crushed my mouth onto hers.

She began to whimper and abruptly pulled back. "Then why don't you put these cuffs behind my back so I can return the favor for what you did to me last night."

Her damp hair felt as silky as her panties when I rubbed it between my fingers, grabbed a fistful and bent her neck back to kiss. Before doing so I asked, "What specifically did I do? As I recall, there was more than one thing."

"You put…you put…" She looked at the floor from where she stood in front of me and bit her lip. "Your mouth on me… down there."

"Oh, Bella." I kissed her neck from top to bottom, pulling the towel away from her and letting it drop to the ground so I could admire the splendor of her nudity. "Very well, little girl."

Unclasping one cuff, I put both her wrists at the base of her spine and locked them there, grabbed a pillow from the bed and placed it in front of her. She took the hint. "You look so pretty on your knees," I told her, petting her cheek with the back of my hand. "Now, open up," It was an order and I dropped my towel, presenting my cock to her mouth. It jerked in front of her face and I took it in my hand to hold it still for her.

"Something tells me you like being the boss of me," she

said and poised those cherry lips in front of my erection, licking her innocent, pink-tongue at the tip of it.

"Oh, yeah?" I said.

"Definitely." She licked again, and the sight of her moist tongue dabbing at me was enough to make me lose it. "Thing is," Bella said, "I'm beginning to realize I love you being in charge."

I growled, unable to wait any more, "Get over here." I used her hair to pull her closer, "Now be a good girl and make me happy."

She lapped around the entire head, and I thought I would come right there. Bella pulled back and asked me, "Does it turn you on, having your prisoner put her mouth on your cock? Keeping her captive and making her service you?"

"Does it turn you on?"

"Definitely, *Daddy.*"

"Well then, princess. That's a yes. Don't I look turned on?" I glanced down at the erect length jutting out from my legs where she was having a hard time fitting it in her mouth. "Looks like you're going to need some help with that. It's too big for you to handle all on your own."

With that I grabbed the back of her head and shoved the first two inches inside of her mouth, which was now stretched wide. She licked the underside and I moaned until she backed off.

She began to nibble up and down my shaft, until she decided to lolly pop lick it from the base to the spot right where the shaft met the head, presenting an incredibly erotic sight for me to enjoy, making me all the more turned on. Presenting my hard-on to her in my hand for her like a present, the skin was taught over its hard interior, and rubbed the tip over those cherry lips, getting my fill of the sight so I could remember it when she was free to go.

When that happened, she would surely leave me. It was

one thing to take pity on a guy you were stuck with, using his weakness against him for a hope at escape. Another matter entirely to remain with that ugly-as-sin individual of your own free will.

No matter, her mouth was driving any regret I had about our little arrangement from my mind. Bella was before me now, and that meant I had a shot at experiencing what it would be like to have a girl like her.

This is what it would be like.

I clasped my fingers behind her neck and held her onto me so that I could fuck her mouth with the tip. Even though I fantasized about her like that, face fucking her so she had to take me further into her mouth… Bella made a preemptive move that shocked the hell out of me.

"Take these cuffs off me, Daddy, I need to touch you. *Please.*"

I quickly unlocked her, and she moved her hands from behind her back to the back of my thighs, using the leverage to pull me further across her tongue, until her eyes watered and she made a little gasping choke, with half of me inside of her mouth and the head touching the back of her throat.

She sucked it, pursing the cherry ring of her lips securely around the shaft, and running her tongue beneath the tip. Her cheeks hollowed when she applied suction, tightening the sensation of pleasure around my cock. At the same time her hands were pumping, and milking my shaft. It was too intense. If I let her continue, I was definitely going to come.

"Bella, get up. Come to bed with me, baby."

"Don't you like that, Daddy?"

"Too much. If you keep it up, I'm gonna come in your mouth. Is that what you want?"

She moaned around me, the vibrating sensation stimulating me to a near unbearable point. I bent down, put my arms around her and tossed her on the bed.

What wanton hussy had taken over me? Having a sex life that was dry as a desert was no excuse for thinking strictly with my lady business. I lusted after Liam like a bunny in round-the-clock heat.

The depravity of it all, cuffed, on my knees, hearing him command, "Look at me." It was as if Liam had control of the handle for the faucet between my legs, all of which he controlled with his gaze (hot), his voice (yum) and his manliness (level ten).

After uncuffing me, he clutched at my head, threading his fingers through my hair to keep me right where he wanted me. He moved his hands around the back of my head, with his thighs on either side of my face and held me still in a vice-like grip. And pumped until he was going to come.

The fact that he backed off and threw me on the bed was disappointing but exciting at the same time. I knew he had the means to drive me over the edge and was eager to see what he had in store now. There was a lot that I've never done before with a guy, and it was weird as fuck that my first experience with so many sexy things was happening while taken captive.

Liam grabbed my ankles and spread me wide, placing lots of little kisses all the way from the bottom of my legs to the inside of my thigh. From time to time, he gave a little lick at my upper legs, as if he was not only okay with my fat, but found it delectable.

"You're so yummy, little girl. I could eat you up all day long."

"Too bad you have to take me to Maryland. If you weren't so strict about that, we could have many more fun times."

His eyes smoldered with intensity when he said, "We'll just have to pack a lot of pleasure into the limited time that we have."

My body tingled all over, but the buzz was most noticeable in my lady parts, and my hardening nipples. I wanted his mouth everywhere and in lieu of saying it out loud, I squealed.

"Fair warning, baby girl." He took a single lap at my clit and my breath caught in my throat. "When you make sounds like that, it makes me want to fuck the shit out of you."

I grabbed his hair in my hands and it was soft and prickly at the same time. It grounded me while he smashed his tongue into my most sensitive place, which made me writhe beneath his mouth and issue pleading keens into the air around us.

That mouth.

His talent. It let me know beyond any shadow of a doubt that I had never been with a real man before. One who knew how to spoil his woman not only by opening her door, carrying her things, protecting her from danger, but by pleasing her enough in the bedroom to make her forget her name.

I didn't forget his though. "Oh Daddy!" I pulled harder on his silky, spiky tresses, "Stop! You're going to make me…"

He shoved two fingers in his mouth, his eyes locked on mine, daring me to look away. With him, it seemed so natural to partake in exchanges that otherwise would make me blush from forehead to sternum.

"Why are you telling me to stop? Obviously you like it. Just hold still for a minute, princess, and let Daddy make you happy."

Make me he did: he made me come so many times I lost count. He made me take all of him in my mouth while holding my hair in his hand—so he could watch me. I was his prisoner; he wouldn't let me get away. And now he was making me do things I wanted to do, but pretended otherwise.

"Get up at the top of the bed and put your hands over your head," he growled.

I decided to poke the bear. "I won't. You can't make me. I'm not your slave!" I slowly crawled up the mattress away from his mesmerizing mouth.

It held me prisoner.

There was something that sparked in his eyes at that point, the recognition that I didn't want him to be gentle. That I needed him to consume me with his maleness. With what he had to offer clothed and unclothed. He yanked on my ankles, pulling me towards him and dove at the throbbing place between my legs.

"I wanted to be soft with you, to lure you to bed and use my mouth to make you beg. But you seem to want it rough." He bit me *there*, not hard enough to hurt, but plenty firm enough to make me see sexy stars. When I thought I could feel no more, he slowly shoved two substantial fingers inside me and began caressing me there.

"Tell me what you want, baby girl. Tell me you want my

cock inside of you now. I'll only give it to you if you let me know what you crave."

He placed his thumb on my clit so that I couldn't formulate a single coherent thought. The only thing I could come up with was, "Yes! Please. Please fuck me."

He stared at the pulsing place between my legs, like a hawk looking down from the sky at a field mouse, and rubbed circles around it with his thumb, "And if I do, are you planning on running away from me? Or are you going to be a good girl and do what Daddy says?"

"I promise to be good. I'll do whatever you say." Pretty sure that people can't be held accountable in a court of law for what they say in the bedroom. His mouth and tongue had me in such a state I would comply with any demand if it meant having him inside me. My need for him was ravenous. Not so much, however, that I didn't hear the familiar warning bells. *Don't let your guard down with him. You know that if you love someone hard enough, they're taken from you in an instant.*

I slid out from him and slowly crawled to the head of the bed like he said, resting my knees on the pillows, creeping my hands up the wall and thrusting my ass back towards him hoping he would give into temptation.

"Ask me to fuck you," he said.

"Daddy, come here and put it inside of me, *please.*" Those were the words that drove Liam past his point of control. He leapt at me, grabbed my hair in his hand to hold himself steady, and placed himself at my entrance. "What are you doing?"

"I'm going to shove it in from behind. Hold still so I can give you what you've been asking for. You're not getting away."

I froze, breathing as if I just returned from a jog. Transfixed and motionless.

Then Liam began to pump, his right forearm wrapped around my chest, lifting my breasts up as he did so. He let my hair fall down my back and grabbed the top of the head board for leverage, using it to drive his fierceness wildly into me, controlling me, possessing me.

He bucked against me, and the way he filled me inside, savagely rubbing against me, meant that while he was chasing his first orgasm, I came again and again and again in his confining embrace. He clutched at my chest and my head, and held me in a vice grip to keep me impaled exactly how he wanted.

"Oh God, your pussy…fuck, it's magic. I'm going to come in you as deep as I can."

He shoved it even deeper, and I wanted to hold him there after he shouted and pulled me tighter, coming his release. I never wanted him to leave.

If only we could have stayed in bed where there was no reward over my head. Where Liam didn't consider me a criminal. Where he was just a man, and I was just a woman. Two people falling in love, or at the very least, lust, and following the feeling where it leads them. But that was not to be.

As we lay in bed before sleep, I didn't know how to tell Liam what I needed to say, and the wolverines in my tummy were wrestling like crazy. He had an inkling of my innocence as conveyed by me, but surely if he knew the whole story he would let me go so I could help my papa. This thing between us had been short, and I was inexperienced. But what Liam and I shared couldn't be commonplace. It felt too right.

Even though my mom's death had taught me it was safer to shelter my heart from loss, rather than give it away to someone, I had to try with Liam. He held me in his big strong arms and I allowed myself to pretend this thing between us was real. In so doing, I convinced myself that it really was.

Real. My big strong daddy would take care of me, and be strict with me when I deserved it.

No matter how hard I tried to warn myself away from it, I could feel my heart tumbling towards Liam faster than I could chase after and catch it.

Tomorrow I'd try and convince him to take my side, and convince him that the people who hired him were up to no good. My freedom depended on it. I fell asleep, and dreamed Liam was my daddy for real, not just a fake one sent to find and capture me, and deliver me to the bad guys.

***

EC-Council: "A hacker's safety may be threatened if they discover vulnerabilities in a system that a nefarious creator wants to stay hidden."

***

The next morning, I washed off and put on my unicorn leggings, soft cotton T-shirt and a pink, fuzzy hoody. Get away clothes or cuddling clothes, depending on how my conversation went with Liam.

We were getting too close to Maryland for my liking, and I didn't have time to fiddle fart around anymore. The keys to the cuffs and the truck were in my sock, in case I had to resort to drastic measures. My secret weapon was tucked into the waist band of my leggings.

The owner of the cottage hadn't secured the safe to anything, relying on it's obscure location in a false bottom of the dresser drawer to keep it secure. Liam stashed his stuff in front of me, not realizing a home safe stored like that could be easily opened, which I did when he was in the shower. All I had to do was drop the safe on the mattress to reset the lock and open it right up. Clearly I watched too many YouTube videos at night.

I let him get dressed before broaching the topic of my innocence since my ability to concentrate didn't stand a chance when faced with his naked, Roman God bod.

Standing between he and the dresser, I made my final plea. "Liam, I know that your employers told you that I could help them solve my father's crime. I'm aware that they accused him of hacking their system when he worked for Bunker, Inc., and I need you to hear me say that it's just not true. The only reason they sent you after me is to find my father who uncovered the fact that *they* were the ones exploiting vulnerable security systems and stealing millions. The people that hired you framed my father for crimes they committed against their own clients!"

His furrowed brow showed me that he was conflicted. He had no reason to believe anything I said when he first met me, but now that we had spent some time together, how could he still consider me a thief? My heart surprised me, pulling tight inside my chest, as if someone was squeezing it in their clenched hand.

How could he want me to call him "daddy" if he actually believed I was a criminal?

"Here's the deal. I know we just met each other, and that things moved pretty quickly between us. You were told I could help your employer nab a criminal, my dad, and yes, I have the skills to do just that—if he *were* a criminal. But I swear to you on all that is holy that I have never committed a cybercrime in my life nor has my father. My Papa raised me right. I became an ethical hacker, like him. His only crime was discovering dirty secrets about the people that hired you."

"Every thief is a troublemaker, Bella. Natural nuisances. Unfortunately for you, you're a problem I've been hired to solve."

Well, that didn't sound like someone who was ready to believe in my innocence. I lowered my eyes and slammed my rainbow striped foot on the carpet.

"Did you just stomp your foot?" he asked, and I wanted to wipe that smirk right off of his face.

"You're not listening to me! What do I have to do to convince you?" I pleaded, recognizing that this was my last chance to convince him and it wasn't going well.

"Precious, I'm afraid there's nothing that you could say that you can say to convince me." He ran his fingers through his wet and wavy hair. "I find myself wanting to cuddle you and protect you from harm. That part is unexpected. But it doesn't mean I can ignore the job I was paid to do. I believe in justice. Right and wrong. You wouldn't like me any other way."

He reached over and twisted a long strand of my hair in his fingers. "I'll be right with you when I take you in and if I suspect the slightest inkling of wrongdoing on their part, and trust me I'll know, we'll be out of there like a shot in the dark."

I took a step away from him. "But why take me there at all!?" I slapped both hands on my thighs.

"Bella, I always finish the job and I'm not about to start being a flake just because I met a pretty girl. You make me laugh, have a banging bod, and feel like someone I could spend an awful lot of time with. Please don't put me in a difficult position. It's very hard for me to resist you when you're being obstinate and cute."

I was pretty sure that if I got naked, I could convince him to let me go. But I didn't have time for that.

He left me no choice. I had run out of options and at the moment I wasn't feeling my cute and sexy factor at all. My focus was on one thing only and there was no way I was going to let him take me in to those corporate hoodlums.

"Well then, I guess there's nothing left to say. Other than I'm really, really sorry." I stared at the carpet and understood what they meant about the heart feeling like a lead balloon. All the joy and tingles Liam made me feel vanished with his stubborn belief that I was lying, and were crushed on the carpet underneath my tennies.

"Hey there, princess." He raised his hand and brushed the back of his knuckles on my cheek, making what I was about to do all the more difficult. But he put me between a rock and his hard body. There was no way I could convince him of my innocence. Left no other choice, I snuck the small can of pepper spray from the back of my waistband. I had lifted it at the gas station mini mart when Liam let me go free.

I blasted him from close quarters and leapt across the mattress to the other side while he was momentarily blinded. Racing to the front door, a ripple of fear trickled down my back when he bellowed, "That's right, little girl. You better run! When I catch up to you, I'm going to blister your behind so badly you won't be able to sit down for a week!"

I kept going, and compelled by my anger at his refusal to think of anything but cash shouted, "We'll see about that! I'll take care of the situation myself, you money grubbing mercenary!"

I slammed the front door behind me. There was still no sign of him following. The pepper spray would completely incapacitate him for a bit. I started the truck and pulled out onto the road.

It was a long way back to my grandma's cabin on Ruth Lake, inland from the Lost Coast back in California. I'd be safe there hiding out, and I'd have time to prove my father's innocence. Then he could come back home where he belonged.

LIAM

ugitive Recovery Agents' Legal Limits: "Prior to transport, all prisoners shall be thoroughly searched for any weapons or contraband."

What an idiot. Allowing her to get close, letting her go for even a moment without handcuffs, because I pitied her. Failing to search her on a regular basis. Even bedding her.

It was my own damn fault.

After half an hour, my eyes still burned, but I could see well enough to set about getting a rental car.

Three days later, I buzzed inland on highway 36, past Bridgeville, headed towards Trinity County. The GPS coordinates told me I was getting closer. My pick up truck had a GPS tracker hidden beneath its carriage. The coordinates took me past Grizzly Creek State Park, where dark green sword ferns painted the banks along the two-lane, windy road.

But the only color I saw was red. *She pepper sprayed me.* Still couldn't believe it.

I knew I was going to have to trek through the woods in

order to find Bella judging by the pin point coordinates broadcast on my tracker.

My schedule was behind due to backtracking to California; I should have been in Maryland by now, collecting my pay to cover the cost of my surgery and a down payment on my fishing cabin. The GPS unit beeped at me an hour and a half off of the 101, letting me know that my truck was parked somewhere down the ridge alongside Ruth Lake, which lay flat below, like an irregularly shaped topaz surrounded by emerald conifers.

Plenty of fishing to do here. Maybe Bella and I really are meant to be together? Did you ever think that this job was fate bringing the two of you together?

I was kidding myself again. No girl like Bella could ever love someone with a face like mine. Wishful thinking wasn't going to get the job done.

I stood, parked in front of a formidable gate which blocked my arrival to wherever my pick up was parked, and God willing, Bella was with it. Once the rental car was parked on the side of the road, I hoofed my way in.

Driving here alone, Bella's absence pulled at my soft underbelly the entire way. I remembered her stupid knock knock jokes—"Orange you glad I'm not a banana?"—the way she scarfed garlic fries. The fact that even though I was her captor and she my prisoner, her outlook on life remained upbeat and entertaining.

Bella didn't fight me like a criminal would; instead, she acted as if our hanging out was the most natural thing in the world. Was she betting on the fact that when I got to know her I'd be compelled to let her go? If so, I'd be damned if she wasn't right about my having second thoughts.

Yes, I was angry that she double crossed me, doused me with pepper spray, and ditched me. But I had to ask myself if that anger was over the fact that she had escaped, or *because she had left me behind*? Climbing over the metal gate hung between two huge stone pillars, I realized I was excited to see her. I had missed her like crazy these past three days.

Her soft, kissable lips.

The brown eyes that looked up at me, peering their way beneath my hard, ugly-assed exterior, reflecting back everything I felt for her like a shadow-dappled pool beneath the trees in the forest.

Her squeezable ass. I imagined hugging her to me and clasping her behind in my hands. My cock swelled as I pictured pulling her closer to me, making her squeal—and I shook my head out of the imaginary spell, telling myself to focus on getting to my truck. And to my baby.

The dirt lane was covered with conifer needles and gravel. The smell of the forest was all around and underfoot, and the fact that Bella took refuge in this untamed place surprised me. How did a young woman whose livelihood meant engaging with a machine for hours, and exploring systems that most people didn't know existed, find comfort in a remote place like this?

It was one more piece of the Bella puzzle that I was determined to solve. My problem was I *always* had a plan. *Always* knew right from wrong. And now that I met Bella, a girl who treated me like a human being and not some monster, a girl who wanted to touch my skin instead of shrink away from it. This young woman had totally disrupted my plan.

And now I planned on disrupting hers.

I stopped at the edge of the clearing and walked into the forest as soon as I saw the road leading to the gray shingled, two-story cabin with white trim. Perfect. I stood back a bit to survey the scene and to make sure Bella didn't have company. My truck was parked in front of the dwelling.

I could have her arrested for auto theft, but I knew damned well I would do no such thing. Instead I worked my way around the cottage, hidden at the edge of the forest. My body was still and quiet like the predator I was: listening, watching, waiting…as I had done a thousand times before on a stake out.

Then I heard it. The sound of my sweet girl singing at the top of her lungs, totally off key. A noise which would make the fur on the back of a cat stand up. Loud. It was so bad, it made me wish for a mute button. She stood at an outdoor sink on the deck, and I watched as she stuck a knife in the soft white underbelly of a trout she must have caught, slid the blade from tail to gills, ripped the guts out and tossed them down under the tan oaks. Right where I was standing. I jumped sideways to avoid the hurling fish guts which swirled straight at me.

Spectacular aim.

Also impressive was Bella's ability to sustain her off-key caterwauling of *Aladdin*'s "Whole New World".

"I can show you the world

Shining, shimmering, splendid

Tell me, princess, now when did you last let your heart decide?"

Though the sound was ear piercing, and cheese-grated my nerves like fingernails scratching a chalkboard, it cracked my daddy core open when she flung her arms wide for emphasis, fish parts in hand, and sung her soul out to the trees, birds, and wilderness. Like the Grinch when he discovered the true meaning of Christmas, I swear, my heart grew three sizes that day.

Then my mind twisted on me, Bella had the *gall* to sing like she hadn't a care in the world. She'd left me behind after pepper spraying me in the face, taking my truck, and hiding away from me. I slowly shook my head while she stood there on a deck in the middle of nowhere, *singing to the chipmunks and blue jays, ignoring me completely*. As if she'd never met me. As if she were better off without me.

I had it bad if I was jealous of forest creatures. Standing there longing to possess her body and soul, enchanted by her terrible performance, I failed to see the second set of entrails flung from her hand for dramatic emphasis, and landing with a splat across my forehead.

I wiped them from my brow, just in time to hear her finish, "On a magic carpet ride…"

"Are you kidding me?!" I shouted and stepped out from the shade of the tree cover. Obviously if she could produce a Disney production in the middle of nowhere without a care in the world, she didn't miss me like I missed her. That was the last thought to cross my mind before I sprang out of the tan oak, leapt up to the deck, and stood between Bella and the back door. "How could you?" I said, and felt a softball in my throat.

Her eyes were big as tomatoes.

"Liam! How did you…?" she asked and dropped her slimy, fish gut covered hands to her sides.

I crossed my arms over my chest to prevent myself from using them to discipline her. "That's a great question. After all, you disabled me with pepper spray, leaving me stranded without a vehicle. Not a single idea where to find you. But for a computer genius you seem a little short on technical expertise. Anybody can purchase a GPS tracking system and put it on the bottom of their car. So thanks for leading me right to you." I towered over her and jabbed my finger at her in accusation.

She did the adorable foot stomping thing again. "Dammit."

Watch your mouth, little girl. I'm short on patience. You need to show me more than a little respect right now unless you're purposefully trying to provoke me and need my hand across your bottom."

Provoke you!? How the hell do you think I felt when you snatched me out of Sacramento and hauled me halfway across the country? Do you think I felt *respected?*"

"I've told you more than once. I was simply doing my job."

"Oh yeah? Well I hate to break it to you, buddy, but your job just became obsolete. So why don't you crawl back into that heartless cave you came out of and leave me alone?"

What are you talking about? Obsolete."

I'm talking about the fact that I've been able to get the data I needed to prove to you for once and for all that I'm innocent and so is my father. Your employers are the ones who are criminals!"

"Oh, yeah? What makes you think that I won't haul your ass in any way?" I wouldn't, of course I wouldn't. She had me reacting just the way she expected. Me, the asshole. The jerk.

Might as well play the part. With the money from this job, I could fix my face. Maybe I'd have a shot with Bella after that. No way she could love a guy like me, looking the way I did.

"Look, I don't expect you to get it, but I need that money. I have no choice but to take you in."

This time she did a bird-like little hop and actually stomped with both feet on the deck. "Ugh! Why did you have to follow me here? I knew you'd never believe me no matter what I said." She threw the trout head toward the pile of entrails where I had stood. Good aim too. "I can't believe I ever felt something for you. You're nothing but a monster!"

Oh Jesus, perhaps it was just an expression. I wanted to believe that when she put her hands over her mouth, fish slime and all, in an effort to shove the hurtful words back inside. She was referring to my behavior. Not the way I looked. Right?

It was just a figure of speech. Still, my stupid heart ached with grief. I couldn't speak and must have looked like a buffalo with an arrow piercing my eye, stunned, still alive, but mortally wounded. I wanted to fall to my knees, wrap my arms around myself and bellow like that injured wild thing. Shout my pain to the mountains so it echoed off the lake and made the water fowl take flight.

The only thing I had to protect me now was my self control. I wouldn't let her see how much she'd hurt me.

"Oh God, Liam. I didn't mean…" Her face was pale as she took two steps towards me.

I waved away her words, staggered by the despair that twisted and turned inside me like a roiling boa constrictor. "Don't worry about it. I know what I am, Bella. It would be stupid for you or me to pretend otherwise."

Picking a stick up off of the deck, I snapped it in two. "I get the impact this has on people." I trailed the sharp twig over the rough side of my face.

The handrail on the stairs off the deck needed repair I noticed as I descended them and headed towards the lake. This entire place could use a little attention.

It wouldn't be getting it from me.

Bella had let it be known how she felt, and I needed to stay in my lane as her captor. She didn't feel the same way towards me as I did towards her, and the open wound of my soul cried out for relief. I had chased her here; she was the first woman in forever that made me feel like a man because of the delight she took in me.

Or so I believed.

She let me know loud and clear—I had no business trying to be her daddy. I jogged down the leafy bank to the cabin's private dock and found a small fishing boat which had the keys in the ignition, got behind the wheel and started her up for a joy ride to the island at the lake's center. I needed some time alone.

It was no small consolation to hear Bella shouting behind me, "Liam! Come back! I didn't mean it that way, please!" But it certainly didn't keep my heart from surrendering in defeat.

It was difficult to breathe, realizing that life without Bella as mine was a reality I couldn't face.

Harder still was accepting that no matter how passionately I had come to care for her, it was time to set her free.

As soon as I heard the roar of the boat motor below the cabin I sprinted to my room and threw on my bikini and river shoes.

I thought I'd be able to catch him on the dock, but by the time I ran to the paved boat launch in front of our place, I saw him pulling away from the shore and heading directly across the lake to the small island. The smell of gasoline fumes was still in the air and I dove headfirst after him.

My lungs constricted and my heart was clogged with guilt. Was it really fair of me to expect him to give up on his dreams just because I asked him to? Would he ever understand that in spite of his scars, he was certainly no monster? He was handsome and kind in my eyes.

But if wealth was his biggest concern was he really a man that I wanted to make mine, or to call my daddy?

No matter what the answer was, I didn't want to hurt him. He couldn't hide from me on the island since I knew every rock, tree, and sand bar. I'd help him see that if we cooperated, I could help him realize his ambition. And get my father back to this country.

When I walked ashore, my toes caught on the marsh grasses that rotted at the edge of the water. There was a small beach with a ring of stones circling the place where a campfire had been built. My boat was tied to the dock but I didn't see Liam anywhere. Luckily it was hot outside so I was plenty warm in just my bikini. I leapt onto the sand.

Where was he?

I walked to the edge of the vegetation bordering the beach, and allowed my eyes to adjust to the dimly lit surroundings. I couldn't hear him or see him and so I cried out his name. "Liam?"

There was no reply so I ventured further into the shadowy, speckled light of the forest. The song of a cicada kicked up nearby, again startling me slightly.

I called out once more. "Hello, Liam?"

"I'm here." The voice was directly behind me and made me jump. I hadn't heard him come up on me.

"Why did you bring the boat to the island?" The bitter flower of shame bloomed across my cheeks when I realized the answer was obvious. I hurt him.

"Why did you swim after me?" Liam never gave me reason to fear him, but when I looked up, his gaze burned with such intensity, I felt my soul shiver.

He stepped towards me and shoved my shoulders down to make me sit on a weathered stump behind me. Instead of expressing anger as I expected, or hurt over my horrible comment earlier, he yanked the bottom string of my bikini top so that if I moved much at all, I'd be sitting on the stump half naked.

"Take it off all the way so I can see your tits," he directed.

Animal hunger took over and made my breasts feel swollen and the place between my legs feel damp.

"Liam!"

"What do you call me?" he said.

I shouldn't like this, not one bit. He was being so different, even more demanding than usual. Tell that to my breath, which now came in soft pants as I eagerly obeyed his command and reached behind my back to untie the top strap around my neck.

I watched his eyes turn dark with desire and realized that he had me right where he wanted me, on the middle of a deserted island without anyone to come to my rescue.

"What do you want me to call you?" I asked.

"You know damn well what I want you to call me." He grabbed my jaw in his powerful hand, forcing me to look up at him, "What I *require* you to call me." He shook my head slightly for emphasis. "What I *command* you to call me."

His bossiness made my nipples rise, diamond-hard and full of desire. "Daddy?"

"That's right. Perhaps you can learn to be a good girl after all." He stepped forward to spear his fingers into my wet hair and I couldn't help but admire the inked bands that circled around his bulging forearms.

I sure as heck shouldn't be enjoying this at all—being required to strip naked in the middle of the forest.

There were so many things that we needed to work out that didn't involve playing sex games in nature. But when he bid me to stand up off of the stump and pulled my bikini bottoms to the ground so I could step out of them, he was all I wanted. All I could think about.

The urgent need to possess Liam could almost be mistaken for well being.

Contentment.

Being carefree.

We stood face to face and pleasure pulsed in my veins. What he would do next?

Liam ripped his T-shirt over his head and laid it down on the stump. "Sit down. Unzip me."

I sat in front of him with his zipper at my eye level and was amazed once more at his thickness. I unzipped him and shoved his jeans over his hips and the blunt head of his erection pressed urgently against my palm as I stroked it.

He was rock hard and ready for me. I pulled down his boxers and used my mouth as a heated cage for his hard on to slide in and out of, flattening my tongue under the sensitive tip.

I began to stroke his shaft and felt it jerk and jump in my hand. Our need for each other was as raw and wild as the woodland in which we stood.

I noticed that every time I slid up his shaft and squeezed at the head, it made him moan out loud as if he were in pain. It made me want him inside of me. My heart began to pound.

He used my throat as a lever to pull my head away from him and said, "Open your mouth wide. I want to watch you make me come."

I'd never experienced anything like this, plunging into submissiveness because I trusted this man to lead the way. When I obeyed, he placed the head of his cock at the entrance to my mouth and I could taste the water droplets on my tongue as he slid it inside.

I was completely filled by him, and he didn't go slowly or gently. Once more, I was surprised by my response to his using force. I opened my mouth to him and took him deeper inside my throat. Eager to please him.

Take it… take it deep." He sounded feral, brutish in his heat, and pushed even farther inside. As odd as it sounded, it calmed me. The fact that he was fucking my throat, snatching all of my control away with his use of me, cleared my mind of all worry.

You look so beautiful with my cock in your mouth. Let's see how you look with my cum painting your pretty lips."

I slid my hand up and down the admirable length of him

and could taste his essence leaking onto my tongue. Surprisingly, it tasted good.

He swelled inside my mouth and my power over him excited me. Who was really in charge here? His body started to buck as I used my fingers to squeeze his shaft. "Say it. Say you want me to come inside your sweet mouth and down your throat."

He pulled away from me and I felt his absence hindering my longing like shackles.

"Please. Please, Daddy, let me be a good girl and make you come."

"That's my sweet princess," he said, petting my hair back and thrusting himself back inside. "You look so pretty with your lips around my cock. Show Daddy how you can swallow every single drop like a good girl."

By now I was rocking back-and-forth on from one butt cheek to the next to release the temperature between my legs where my pussy was pulsing its heat.

Maybe I'll just keep you out here forever where no one can find you and make you my little sex toy. Would you like that? The big horrible monster and his sweet, innocent, cock sucking princess? Do you think this monster will be able to keep you happy out here in the middle of nowhere?"

Liam's words excited me further and I was surprised at my response to his naughty fantasy. In fact, the thought of being his prisoner in and of itself got me hot. But there was one thing I had to set straight. "You're no monster, Liam."

What if he wasn't play acting? What if he *didn't* let me go? The fantasies were messing with my head—and my lady business. I was soaking Liam's T-shirt beneath me.

He surprised me again by demanding my complete submission. "Take it all the way down your throat!" he snarled, shoving himself as far as he could. But I didn't choke.

It was as if I were made to suck Liam. The harder he fucked my face, the more I wanted it inside my mouth.

He grabbed both sides of my head, and shoved himself all the way inside, warning me, "Here it comes. Swallow. Swallow it all like a good fucking girl and then me off with your tongue. Get every drop."

I swallowed it all and was now reveling in the fact that he was still as hard as when we started. "What did I say?"

It seemed this was payback for having hurt him on the deck, and I attempted to make it up to him by making a show of looking up into his eyes and licked every drop from his gorgeous erection, anxious to taste him further.

He gently stroked the side of my face. Bringing me back to reality, he wove his fingers in my hair to gently guide me to him. "That's right, let me see you suck the head clean, like a good girl."

I took all of him in my mouth and sucked him clean. Oddly, I felt so proud of myself, and more love and cared for than ever when Liam stroked my wet hair and told me again, "You're such a good girl, and you're *mine*."

I probably should have been upset but realized that there was some part of me deeply turned on by behaving according to his will. If he said "suck" I'd ask, "How hard?". It wasn't as if I were hurting anyone. I was simply enjoying a carnal animalistic moment and allowing Liam to dominate and control me.

Nothing had ever felt so right.

"Put your knees up on that stump and spread your legs for me," he said, and I felt the rough heat of his hands on me.

At this point I would do anything he told me, and it wasn't in order to seek escape or trick him into believing something that wasn't truly there. I did this because I needed to. Liam fulfilled something inside me that had been missing and I didn't even know it.

When I was with him I felt safe and unbroken. His power grounded me, protected me from everything but him. It was what I needed.

"That is a gorgeous site, precious." He ran his hand up my thigh. "Never in a million years did I think that being hired for a job would lead me to something as sweet as you." He placed two fingers over my clit and then began to firmly draw circles around it until I lost it.

I moaned and he stopped.

"You're so wet, baby girl. And it's sticky wet. I don't think it's from the lake. Did sucking my cock get you excited?" He moved in front of me so that again his crotch was right at mouth level, put his fingers beneath my chin and lifted it so I was forced to look up at him while he cleaned my essence from his fingers like frosting.

"Tell me how badly you want it." He clenched his hand in my hair.

It made me want to rub up against his leg like a kitten.

It was obvious he had me in his spell. I wasn't going anywhere and remained of my own accord.

Could I really be considered his captive, if I wanted to be trapped by him?

At this point there was no excuse. I knew fucking her was wrong. She called me a "monster" and dipping my dick into her pussy showed an absolute lack of self-respect on my part, and at the same time, I knew I'd risk everything, including my pride, just to have her again.

God forgive me, there was no way I could resist tracing the delicate softness of her lower lips.

I pulled her towards me so I could reach her; my kisses were greedy when I adored her mouth with my tongue. It was important she felt how hungry she made me, and how overpowering was the pulse that throbbed in my veins; a scarlet web of desire.

She needed to feel pain in a way that was hard to endure —not the suffering of war, but the misery of unfulfilled passion. I'd torture her with my mouth until she trembled with desire.

Slipping my belt from my jeans, I grabbed both of her wrists in one hand. "I changed my mind. Lay over that stump across my T-shirt like a good girl and show me that supple, juicy ass."

She did as she was told and made a begging sound when I gently caressed her round and full with the belt. "I told you not to run away. I told you I would take care of you and to make things right. But did you listen?"

As if goading me in order to receive my punishment she responded, "No, Daddy, I didn't listen. I was a very bad girl."

My eyes did not deceive me—she lifted that lush ass towards the tree canopy and presented herself more fully to my cock. Although I had intended to discipline her, watching her respond this way made me think of only one thing, and that was how badly I needed to fuck her.

But first things first. "Don't make any noise until I tell you that you can."

I raised my arm in the air and brought the belt down on her ass, watching her flinch beneath the sound of the leather whipping through the air.

She scrabbled a bit on her feet and her toes kicked up the forest duff made hot by summer's breath. I placed my foot on her back and held her in place for ten more blows. She received those without crying out. When I laid into her with the eleventh blow, I gave her permission to make a sound.

Daddy, please. I'll be good, I swear it. Please stop spanking me. It hurts so badly." She began to keen and beg in a way that fed my hunger.

Upon the twentieth swat I asked, "Are you certain you can be a good girl and obey me from here on out?"

Yes, Daddy, I promise!"

She was wet and weeping between her legs when I stroked her with my fingers.

I leaned down to inhale the scent of her hair at the nape of her neck, and she bit back a whimper. The beast in me stamped the earth with its cloven hooves, preparing to descend on the helpless and tempting girl beneath me who was now thrusting her behind at me, daring me to take her.

"Is that anyway for a good girl to behave? Do you think a good girl would be so wet from her daddy's spankings? Pumping her hips up at him?"

"No, Daddy. I think I'm a very, very bad girl and need to be taught a lesson. I think you must punish me with that big dick of yours."

She was definitely playing with fire. I reached down to pump my hard flesh, which strained toward her, aching for release and said, "You're to ask permission before you come. Understand?"

I made her stand again and was overpowered by the temptation of her lips. My kiss was greedy and untamed. Uncontrollable and overpowering; I tried to push it back and to keep the savage inside me at bay, prevent it from clutching at Bella with relentless, snatching claws.

When I lifted my lips away from her face she surprised me and leaned against my chest with a sigh of contentment. As if she had no idea of the beastly urges that coursed through me.

As if she felt safe with me.

Her voluptuous body and her tight nipples tempted me, and I grabbed them between my fingers and twisted slightly. I pulled her towards me and placed my mouth over one nipple while twisting the other with my thumb and index finger. Her breath became ragged, and stoked an animal hunger in me so that my shaft drove upward in a thick curve.

The thought of those pouting lips around it while fucking her pretty mouth wasn't enough.

I needed to have her pussy.

I drew her towards the stump again and had her kneel on top of it, drawing a line through the folds of her soaking wetness. My princess was ready for her beast. I could smell her arousal, and began to rub her clit with my thumb, making sure she's ready to take all of me. "Let me hear you beg for it."

With the belt still in my hands I slipped it over her neck and pulled her very gently backwards onto my stiff erection and buried myself fully inside of her. Her back arched in response to being fucked.

I grabbed her shoulders with my hands, pulling her backwards onto me so she rode me up and down as I thrust her hard from behind. I wasn't gentle. I rode her like a brute and now and again I tugged the belt to pull her back towards me.

"Do you want to run away from me?" I bent down and whispered into her ear. "You think I'm an animal with this face?" I gritted my teeth, and the thought of Bella's disdain for me made my voice grow cold in fear of her disapproval, that which gnawed at me since she ran away. "You hate what I look like?"

"No! Daddy, I feel safe with you. Protected." She leaned back into me when I snapped my hips at her in approval, rewarding her by pumping my savage flesh into her, and felt my male pride swell to hear her hum in satisfaction.

"I *love* you, Liam! I love being with you." Convulsive waves gripped her and squeezed around me.

Her words made me wonder about this thing called luck. One day my luck could be so bad as to put me in the middle of a tank fire and burn my face off, and years later I was alongside Bella, who gave me hope that just because my past was shit, it didn't mean my future couldn't be better than I imagined. And she *loved* me?

For the first time since my accident I felt attractive, as if Bella had broken some kind of spell which kept me trapped in my own blinding insecurity.

How did I get so lucky as to have Bella walk into my life and change my world completely? Instead of saying those flowery and affectionate words to her, all I could think to say was, "Go ahead. Ride that thing like you want to tame it, little girl. Break that beast."

She whined at my dirty command and I placed my hands on either side of her hips to pull her onto me harder. "Use your words, baby girl. Tell Daddy. Do you want this?"

"Oh, yes, Daddy. Fuck me," she mewled. She rose up on her knees. It made me feel powerful to wrap one arm across her chest and use the other to rub her clit.

"That's right. You need to come again, baby girl." I pinched at her swollen clit and she moaned so loudly that my cock began to throb inside her. I felt her pussy clamp down around me and I grit my teeth against the oncoming release.

I kept talking to her because fuck if it didn't make me horny. "That's what you needed, wasn't it? Me fucking you hard, and making that little pussy bow down to me?" Slam. "Show her who's boss?" Slam. I moved my forearm around her ribs, setting her tits free so I could watch them jiggle from over her shoulder as I slammed into her, twisting her nipples with the other hand.

The feel of her weighty, pretty breasts bouncing in time to my savage thrusts was too much. I held her hips, while we bucked and thrashed against each other in shared release, then pulled her onto me, resting fully inside her pulsing pussy while my cock surged into her.

I was still semi-hard as I stood panting above her, gradually becoming aware of our surroundings again. The buzz of a cicada, the squawk of a blue Jay, and the chirpy bark of a chipmunk and the sound of waves splashing the shore.

Bella was supposed to be my captive, and yet she had unexpectedly imprisoned my heart along the way. I didn't expect our intimacy to be as wild and uninhibited as this place, and I realized I had been a fool to try and take her in.

"Can I give you a lift?" Liam asked me after we were dressed. Unexpectedly, he swooped his arm under my bum, scooped me off the ground and carried me to the boat which floated a short way off shore.

"Liam! I can walk, you know. I do it all the time."

He laughed as if he found me delightful, and I realized I had never heard him sound so carefree. His smile was lazy, like a Sunday afternoon. "Can't have my princess walking in pond splooge now, can I?"

"Pond splooge?" I repeated. "Is that a scientific term?" I realized that I had grown to love looking at his face, his scars were as handsome to me as the most unflawed and traditionally handsome features on the planet, because they belonged to him, and I thought of him as *mine*.

"Are you hungry?" I raised myself over the buzz of the small engine propelling us back to the cabin, loving the familiar way the cooler air above the lake swept past us, light as our mood.

"Ravenous," he said. "For dinner, and for you."

I followed Liam up the plank of the small dock after he

tied up the boat and he reached back for my hand. It was odd.

Something had shifted between us.

Now that the afterglow had time to dissipate I thought about how I had said "I love you," and Liam didn't say it back. Every expectant lover's worst nightmare. And yet, I wasn't crushed. I could sense his feelings for me, and they went beyond lust. It may be true that I started out as a business transaction for him, but he had come to care for me.

Something was holding him back from admitting how much, but I felt wanted with him. Waiting for him to admit he loved me wasn't the hardest thing I'd ever done. I'd been waiting for my papa to come home, waited for my mama's life to run out, waited to find the key to put corporate crooks in jail.

I heard my mama's words in my head but they were of little consolation. "Don't be a woman that needs a man. Be a woman a man needs."

Feeding my tummy was a good distraction. I was starving and there were two fresh, fat trout in the fridge. I'd concentrate on dinner, and ignore the awkward things unsaid between us. Hot tears welled up behind my eyes, lapping at the roots of my lashes like boat wake on the shore below. I *wouldn't* cry, in spite of the emotional wreck I had suddenly become.

Flipping on the tiny radio that had sat on the kitchen window sill since dinosaurs roamed the earth, I dialed into BBC news, "...and in a shocking reversal of events, the CEO of Bunker Inc. was identified today as the mastermind behind the hijacking of bank data for over one hundred corporations..."

Bunker was the company my dad and I had been investigating. I cranked up the volume. Bunker Inc. was the firm that hired Liam to apprehend me.

"Earlier this year, the CEO, Andrew Smurton, reported the data breach of client banking accounts and accused international hackers for said cyber attack. Contradictory evidence, allegedly coming from a private source, has resulted in Smurton being taken into custody."

Dad! He must have beat me to solving the puzzle of how to prove Smurton was behind it all along. "According to our sources, evidence includes indisputable proof of abnormal bank transfers which were ordered from *within* Bunker Inc. The financial impact of the breach is as yet unquantified but is anticipated to be over $50 million. The judge in Smurton's case has determined that he is a flight risk for pretrial release, and therefore, no bail has been set."

I turned to Liam, who was taking his shoes off at the door and heard it all. Overwhelmed by what we just heard, he moved to the dining table and collapsed into a chair. The color drained out of his face.

"What's the matter? This is good news, right? It proves I'm innocent and my papa can return home now."

He wouldn't look at me, and blew out a long, low sigh.

With a thickening voice that almost cracked as he spoke he said, "I'm glad you're happy, Bella, and I'm happy for you. It's just sinking in that my only hope for having surgery to mend my face and making myself worthy of your love has just slipped through my hands."

It was suddenly hard to breath and my chest tingled. "What good would the money be if I were a prisoner of those goons?"

"It's illogical; I get it." Liam shook his head, muttering, "Of course right now you think it will be all better, but I have to wonder, how long before you look at me and realize you're with, to use your words, 'a monster?'"

I gasped, and gaped at him like the fish I was about to cook for dinner. "Liam, it's just an expression, not a reference to the way you look. I told you earlier I love you and I meant it!" The anguish I felt over my stupid slip of the tongue and how badly it hurt him stabbed me like a knife.

He had to believe we belonged together, no matter what war had done to his face.

"When you ran away from me and I came after you, it was for personal reasons, Bella. I had three days to realize there was no way I could deliver you to Smurton. After spending time with you, I knew you weren't lying about his being a crook. But I know what I look like, Bella, and I worry you'll tire of it eventually."

I cried and kissed the rivulets of scars on his left side pausing to say, "You are the most handsome man I've ever seen, inside and out. It's the inside bit that matters most to me, and now that we can be together, everything will be alright."

"I guess that's what I'm coming to terms with, precious." He looked at me and I saw my heart reflected in his tender gaze. "I used to want a normal face more than anything. Now what I figured out is the only person I care about pleasing is you. If you're attracted to me looking like this…" his smile was pure male, "… then fuck it. I'd set myself on fire all over again and wear the scars of damage on my entire body for the chance to be with you for life." He picked me up off the ground and spun me in a circle, "The moment has come for me to confess… I love you, Bella. I think I have since that morning you ordered a Big Rigger for breakfast."

BELLA

Four Months Later

"*H*allllllp! I need help getting this dang thing shut!" I put my knee on the center of my suitcase and used all of my weight to press it shut, but the unwieldy thing wasn't cooperating to zip closed.

Liam leaned against the frame of the bedroom door and spoke. "You're too little to do it by yourself; let me help you." Of course getting my bag shut was no problem for Liam. "Come on, Bella, you have everything that you need and if you need something else you can buy it when we get there!"

My kindle was loaded with what I hoped would be enough books for the three months we planned to spend in Cuba: enough time to meet papa's new love, for Liam to have his facial reconstructive surgery, and to vacation and act like tourists.

An unwillingness to leave the cabin was setting in. It made no sense; I was excited to go, but I couldn't control the urge to assume the plane would go down in flames and Liam's surgery would end with him worse off than when he started. "I can't help it, I've never been out of the country before, let alone to Cuba. "

Liam grunted exaggeratedly when he lifted my bag off the bed and I walked to the bathroom while twisting a long strand of hair around my fingers, and emptied my bladder for the third time.

Too much coffee. Finishing up, I entered the hallway and ran smack dab into Liam, who took the two sides of my fact between his hands. *"Hey."*

"Hey," I answered, trying to memorize what he looked like since the face before me, which I had grown to love, was going away.

"It's gonna be okay," he soothed, "and you've definitely had enough coffee for today." He ran his fingers through my hair and gave it just a bit of a tug. "The worst of this is behind us. Smurton is locked up. I'm all set with a great surgeon, and I'll be holding your hand the entire way on the plane."

"That's easy for you to say. You've been overseas a million times."

"That's right, it's old hat to me. Daddy will take care of you the entire way."

I covered my face and peeked through my fingers at him. It still made me shy sometimes when he called himself my "daddy".

"Come here, Princess. You're so adorable." He moved closer and ground himself up against me, and I would never tire of the way his body radiated a raw and primal strength, and that included the hard thickness which he rubbed against me. "You made me like this. I can't be around you without getting hard. How am I going to survive this trip without putting my mouth on you?"

"Come on, Daddy; if we don't leave for the airport now, we'll be late."

"Isabella Tate, are you even listening to me?" Liam's hands were on his hips, and his chin jut out from his neck.

Honestly, if he was talking to me, I hadn't heard a word he said. There was so much to see in the San Francisco airport: candy stores, express spas where you could get a massage and your nails done, book stores, and fancy coffee shops.

"I'm sorry, I was distracted by all the bright and shiny stuff. What'd you say?" I asked, eyeballing an iridescent unicorn backpack in a display window.

"I said I'm starving and we have an hour to board the plane. That place looks nice." He grabbed my hand and somehow managed to carry my pillow, my fluffy throw and my carry on bag in his other hand.

He led me to the restaurant which had high backed bench seating in tufted grey velvet, sheepskin pillows and the walls were lined with vertical wooden slats for a cozy effect. I took the bench seat and Liam sat beside me asking, "What are you having?"

Passenger names were announced loudly over the intercom so I pointed to the "Truckstop Deluxe: Always meat, often potatoes, rarely vegetables," and a glass of Pinot Grigio, Alois Lageder Alto Adige, Italy 2018 because hey, I could be down home and classy at the same time.

The waiter arrived, and Liam ordered for both of us. We had fallen into an easy pattern of his ordering for me every time we went out and I secretly loved it, but liked to tease him that he was old fashion and definitely born a century too late. Liam wrapped my fluffy throw with huge pom-poms around my shoulders after taking care of business, and snuggling kept me cozy and secure. As much as possible anyway.

"Are *you* nervous?" I asked Liam.

We had only been together four months, but there were so many things Liam understood about me better than I understood myself. He told me there was nothing wrong with feeling afraid or anxious, that he felt that way all the time when he was down range and even after. The main thing, he said, was identifying the soothing activities that calmed your mind.

Such coping skills could tame the snapping fangs of unease or worry when they rose their ugly heads. Liam encouraged me to find a therapist so I could work on the difficulty I had feeling truly out of harm's way. Since Mama died, I was vigilant, and watched out for myself and my papa. Fearing always that the other shoe would drop and that our well-being would be disrupted by some unknown threat.

I had Liam to protect me now.

He told me it was his job to make sure everything was okay, and took care of all the icky grown-up distractions which I was perfectly capable of but hated so much:

- paying bills
- grocery shopping and cooking
- paying taxes
- Etc., etc., etc.

Liam said I had been a grown up for too long and deserved some carefree time so I could focus on starting up my new White Hat Hacker company. Besides, he said, he liked being in charge.

Liam took a sip of his IPA and said, "The thing that worries me the most is having an operation in a country that I'm not familiar with. But like you said, we've done the research, found the best surgeon, and the medical care in Cuba is amazing. Trust me, I've been through a lot worse than being under the knife with anesthesia." He tapped his fingers on the table and flicked his eyes towards the kitchen. "Besides, they can't make this face any worse."

I placed my hand over his huge paw. It was three times the size of mine which never failed to blow me away.

And make me want him in his mouth.

"Liam, you know that I love you no matter what. It's not too late to change your mind. You don't have to have this operation for me."

"Yes, I do, Bella. I'll never feel good enough for you, I'll never be the man that you deserve if I don't at least *try* to have this surgery."

He picked up my wine glass and held it to my lips so that I could have a sip and I could feel the hot tears well behind my eyes. "I don't know what to say right now." I had no idea there was a reward for putting Smurton behind bars. Papa called me up as soon as he was aware and let me know he would split the six million dollars, posted by numerous companies as a reward for the safe return of proprietary information which had been hacked.

Papa insisted on splitting the reward since he wouldn't have been able to stop and freeze the infiltration without my help. My specialization in penetration testing helped discover vulnerabilities in Bunker's infrastructure, ID the avenues used to cyberattack client accounts, and block those pathways harder than a Network firewall.

My father had fled to a small town just outside of Havana on the Carribean coast, since Cuba had no extradition rights. He told me it was possible to find an excellent surgeon for Liam for a fraction of US healthcare costs, and Liam insisted on paying for it himself.

Not only would Liam and I be spending a nice vacation on the beach, I would be reunited with my papa.

Liam put his steady hand over my fidgety one and said, "I'll be back in a couple of minutes, Princess. I'm going to get a magazine or book to be at that shop over there. Do you want anything?"

I continued to tear and roll sugar packets up into pea sized pellets, stacking them into pyramids. "I'm good, Daddy. Thank you for taking such good care of me." I watched as Liam crossed the airport hallway to the news shop across the way. It was amusing to watch the shop girl track his movements through the store.

Although Liam didn't realize it, he was extremely striking and women followed his huge, hulking form with covetous eyes wherever we went. I found it to be a bit of a turn on, and marveled again at the luck I had running into him while running away from the people who were trying to incriminate my father. Liam returned with a hardback novel in his hands for me and placed it on the table, *The Sleeping Beauty Trilogy Box Set* by Anne Rice.

"What's this?" I asked.

"A little something to make sure you'll be thinking of me when I'm in the hospital and you're laying on the beach. Pick your scene, baby girl. Daddy will give it to you when he gets out."

I leaned against Liam's chest with a sigh of contentment when he slid in next to me on the bench. How many women were lucky enough to have a partner that bought them books? Many a time, he had benefited from my intense need stoked by the heat between the pages of a romance book I was reading. Still, Liam surprised me by bringing me this book, written in the eighties, and promising me it would make me feel like doing naughty things with him.

Since his last job didn't pan out, aka. me, Liam decided to purchase the piece of land next to our cabin. Using his savings, he began investing in real estate around the lake, renovating old properties and turning them into Airbnbs. I could work remotely and we loved living next to the lake.

I sat next to my papa, baking under the warm sun on Playa Los Pinos.

Liam hadn't let me visit him in the hospital, and it was driving me crazy not to see him every day and not knowing how he was doing. Whether he was in pain. Whether he had enough to eat or drink.

I distracted myself calling out to Paco, who ran the bar and restaurant of sorts on the beach. The food was amazing, but most Americans would not consider it to be an actual restaurant. But because I could get grilled lobster for ten dollars, brought directly to my place on the playa, I was in the habit of ordering it every day.

Paco would bring it to me with a piña colada, rice and fresh fruits. I had never experienced such luxury in my life, and I had grown accustomed to the locals on this beach calling me "guitarra".

Which meant "guitar". It was supposed to be a compliment because it meant that my body was shaped like a guitar, in other words an hourglass figure but perhaps a bit more well-rounded.

After eating a late lunch Papa and I sat in silence on our chaise lounges and read our books. As per usual, this ended in our dozing off and taking an afternoon siesta.

I started awake from sensing that some large body sat next to me at the end of my chaise, and my eyes landed on him. I knew it was him, his sheer size, the familiar half of his face, but he looked much different, "Liam! You look different, but the same. I'm so glad you're still you." My pulse quickened.

"Yes, silly. I'm still me. There were parts of my face so damaged, I wanted them repaired. My drooping eye for example, but what you said to me in the airport, the way you love me the way I am, those things made me change my mind. I realized that I didn't need to try to erase all of the damage. So long as you find me attractive, I feel like the best looking guy on the planet. I hope you don't mind that a few scars remain."

"They make you look dangerous. Like a warrior." I said.

Liam cupped both sides of my face and gave my lower lip a hungry nibble. "Let's take a little walk, shall we?"

My papa waved us away in a "you kids go have fun" gesture.

I don't know why I was suddenly shy, but although I had the impulse to stare at and inspect his new features, shyness won out. As if I couldn't look at him. Luckily, Liam took my hand and pulled me off the chaise lounge. As we walked hand in hand, he began talking to me.

"I used to take the little things for granted, Bella. My looks. Being able to walk down the street without freaking people out," he flung his left hand in front of him, "but I'll tell you one thing I'll never take for granted in a million years, and that's the day I met you. You're the greatest gift I've ever received and it means everything to me to be your daddy. To care for you and protect you."

The beach was deserted at this end of the strand and we kept going. "You put the pieces of me back together, made me whole, and I never want to be without you again. These past two weeks in the hospital were hell without you. I missed your singing, your laugh, you stomping your feet. All of the unique things that make Bella my beauty, inside and out. How I've missed you."

We rounded the point and the turquoise sea was beginning to catch the changing light of the sun, the palm trees bordered the beach immobile in the still air.

And Liam got down on one knee.

"What are you doing, Liam?" Now I could look at him.

My Liam, slightly different in aspect but he radiated the same soul and charismatic strength from his features.

I had grown to love his former looks, and this new face, albeit more conventionally handsome, would take some getting used to. As if he read my mind, he looked up at me and said, "I've got a fake ear, a rebuilt scalp and a fixed eyelid." He drug his fingers over his eye and cheek which no longer drooped and pulled unnaturally tight over his bones.

"In spite of all that, Bella, my heart is the realest you'll ever find." From his back pocket he pulled out a black velvet box, which he opened, presenting to me a diamond ring whose size improperly unhinged my jaw so you could shove a tangerine inside my mouth.

"You've taught me how to love, Bella. Please say you'll share a lifetime of adventures with me. Marry me, please."

I flung myself at him, and he allowed himself to fall back on the sand so that I could kiss him hard, then soft, then hard again. "Oh Liam, I never want to be without you. Your time in the hospital let me know that. Don't you ever do anything like that to me ever again!"

I felt his kiss tingling in my bones, "Yes, I will marry you. You're my fairytale come true."

EPILOGUE

"This is so kinky." Lord knows Liam and I had traveled every corner of the globe when it came to our sex life, but surprisingly he never made me do this. "Where did you get the blindfold?"

At the gate to the cabin, he parked and insisted on tying a silk fabric over my eyes. Once there, he let me out of his pick up, okay, "our pick up" he would correct me, and pulled me along by the wrist.

Liam had hinted while we were in Cuba that there was a surprise in store for me when we returned to the cabin and finally I would get to see what all the secrecy was about. "Is this really necessary? Can't I just see it now?"

"Quit chattering." Liam ground up against my bum and said, "Focus on what looking at your bottom makes me want to do." He ground into me again. "You made me like this."

There was absolutely no mistaking that he was hard. "Okay; don't get your panties in a wad. I was just wondering how you happen to have a silk blindfold on hand."

Every sound, scent and touch was amplified. Standing on the deck, I heard insects buzzing, and smelled the sun-heated

123

earth. Liam opened the front door for me and took my hand to lead me down the hallway. It went on for much further than I remembered. The cabin was modest in size, but had been expanded while we were gone and I was walking on carpet that wasn't there before.

"What's this?" I asked, pointing downwards to the floor.

He stopped me by grasping my shoulders under his heated palms and kissed me as though it was the only way he could stay alive. Grabbing my chin, he stroked up the sides of my face, down again to the back of my neck and told me without words I was loved: beginning slowly and then claimed my mouth with a savage kiss.

"Can I take the blindfold off now?" I asked.

"Don't you dare. I'll let you know when you may take it off. Now come *here.*"

Liam took my hand in his huge one, and deftly led me across an unfamiliar floor, set me down on an overstuffed chair that had never been there before and I asked, "Okay now what?"

"One of these days, little girl, your persistent inquisitiveness is going to get you in trouble. But not today." I could hear the crackly sound of him unfolding a piece of paper, and then he cleared his throat, "I wrote something for you.

Fear Not

His damage didn't scare her, nor the wounds that scarred his flesh,

No one but her could love him and the demons stirring beneath his chest.

She did not fear his gloom, or the devil who
leapt in his eyes...

He knew no one would ever love him with what lie awake inside,

Familiar with what the bowels of hell were -
how could anyone understand?

But she shone her light upon him, and the beast became a man."

I fidgeted in the chair; Liam had never read me any poem that he had written. "You *wrote* that?"

"I did. It's an ode to you." His deep voice seemed to fill the room more than usual with my eyes covered and I could feel my nipples go tight. Poetry and brawn, a dangerous and panty-dropping combination. "I'm hoping it will get you horny."

"Hmmm, well, you're in luck."

He slid his hands up the outside of each leg, and peeled off my panties along with my pants, then picked up my hand in his and led me across the room. "Sit down here." He guided me to sit on a rung. "Put your hands behind you to grab the poles on either side." Liam lifted my heel up on a lower ladder rung, and one leg bowed open so that the lash of his tongue kept me prisoner to desire, pinned between the ladder and his mouth.

He squeezed together the entire span of my lower lips in a single hand and began licking my pinched together hood up and down. My entire body began to vibrate in response and I had a hard time staying on that ladder. Liam grabbed the back of my left thigh for support, and continued his magical tricks with the help of his other hand and his mouth.

Taking a hint, he began to squeeze at me harder and nibble and suck at me with more force so that the rough motion sent me over the edge. He rose up and covered my mouth with his to swallow my every whimper.

Although I was still blinded, I knew my beast was cunning, and he wasn't done with me yet.

I was right.

Liam scooped me up in his arms and carried me to another part of the room, set my bare feet on the carpet, and bent me over at the waist so that the side of my face was laying on the cool, slick surface of a desk. "Put your hands above your head and don't lower them until I instruct you to."

He used his booted shoe to drive my bare feet apart. "Spread your legs for me, precious, let me show how much I love you. In other words, you're completely at my mercy, kitten, and I intend to make you purr."

I could hear the assertive unzip of his trousers and the rustle of material as he took off his pants, and the thud of him kicking his shoes off. "Something tells me you need it rough today. Is Daddy right about that, precious?" For emphasis, he pressed up against me from behind, so that his hairy, muscular thighs teased me.

And of course there was that impressive reminder of his desire, probing my wetness. I wanted him to split me in two with it.

It was impossible to see, but I could sense him raising his arm and his gigantic palm came down hard on my bottom. I winced, belying my next words which were intended to goad him on. "Didn't hurt!"

"Stay still," he said.

"Like I have a choice. You're bigger, stronger, and faster than me!" I sassed and then yelped as he promptly slapped my bottom again.

"What were you saying?" he asked, hand poised, and I decided to keep my mouth shut so as not to distract him from my primary objective.

To make him pound me like a jackhammer.

Instead, his cock teased me, rubbing without entering, until I writhed for him, senseless and submissive.

"Hot little thing, aren't you," he said. "Let's see if this helps cool things down." He cracked his hand down upon my ass again. "Someone needs to be reminded who's in charge. Who's in charge, precious?"

"You are, Daddy!" I opened my legs wider to encourage him, reaching back to try and grab his shaft.

"Ah, ah, ahhh. Hands to yourself." With that he lifted me by the ass cheeks, shoving my belly up on the slick surface so that I barely caught myself on my forearms and he ordered me to display myself. "Reach back and pull yourself apart to show me how much you love me, precious."

His enormous fingers were on me again, rubbing me hard in just the right spot, stoking my shivers of ecstasy again as I moved my lips apart.

Liam's heavy and erect thickness touched me and then shoved inside a little. "Is that what you want, my greedy girl?" All I could do was make a frustrated sound at the back of my throat.

He pushed further. "So. Tight." Not a single shove but a series of small nudges designed to tease me, each one thrusting him slightly deeper, filling me slowly, until he gave one final push and I could feel his groin slapping against me.

His hands moved from my hips and slapped over my breasts, lifting me onto his throbbing cock so that I was nearly hanging off of him.

My erect nipples poked out between his fingers, and he brought them together, to squeeze hard and roughly rub them.

I started to rotate my hips in slow circles around him, while he continued to shove inside of me, chasing his pleasure and stoking mine at the same time.

Liam rode me hard, moving his hands from my breasts to the top of my wrists, pinning me down and my excitement blazed higher. My tormented groan begged him to continue. "Yes, Daddy. Fuck me. I want you to come in me!"

Those were the magic words. Liam sounded feral, brutish in his heat. "You little savage. You love it when Daddy traps you and fucks you hard, don't you."

The sound of sweat-slick skin slapping together filled the room and while Liam filled me with his throbbing erection, he leaned down to mark me as his, biting the back of my neck as he moved hard and fast, jackhammering toward a desperate climax, and our bodies fused in one shared hot, sticky release.

"Am I allowed to take off my blindfold yet?" The suspense was killing me.

"I don't know; after your response today, I might make you wear this thing 24/7."

"Very funny, Liam. I did what you said, now can I please see what you did?" I let my caress play over his hard pecs and the fuzzy hair there that I loved.

"I guess you have been a very, very good girl for Daddy. Are you ready?" he asked

"Yes; please, please let me take it off." I tugged at the ties and the silk blindfold fell to my lap. I blinked rapidly, to prove to myself that what I was seeing was real.

All around me, organized in decorative stacks by color, were all the books I'd collected throughout the years, waiting in boxes until I had enough shelves to display them. But I never imagined anything as beautiful as this. "But how did you… how did you know?"

"It's my job to know everything about you, precious. What kind of daddy would I be if I didn't? I'd be just any other guy and you're worth way more than that."

I spun around, admiring all the things I couldn't see while Liam was ravishing me to planet orgasm. The oriental rug with tones of pink, turquoise, and beige. A ceiling fancier than any I'd lived with, some sort of coppery metallic print, covered with a pattern of octagons and squares made of mahogany. A beautiful painting above a marble fireplace. "Wait a minute. Is that the…"

"It is. The flat rocks in Utah next to the Airbnb where we first…"

"Where you first spanked me!"

He raised a saucy and cocky brow at me. "Are you saying you didn't like it, little girl?"

I scuffed my bare foot on the soft carpet. "No. I'm not saying that." My cheeks heated up. Liam could still quell me in a hot second with his stern daddy tone of voice. How could something make me bashful and horny at the same time? "I can't believe you put in a library ladder; it's a dream come true! You're going to spoil me with all of these surprises."

He stroked me with his eyes. "You know what happens to spoiled little girls don't you?"

I slowly nodded my head, knowing very well what was in store for naughty girls but wanting to hear him say it anyway.

His eyes turned dark with desire. "They get spanked." He picked up my left hand, the one with the fat diamond on it, and kissed me.

A few things dawned on me all at once: my body felt deliciously sore; Liam made me feel wanted, loved, and esteemed; and he chose me out of all the girls in the world. He made me feel precious, just like he had been calling me all along.

REVIEWS

Reader reviews can make a *huge* difference for an indie author. If you enjoyed this book, taking three minutes to leave honest feedback will help a great deal. Thank you!!!

https://www.amazon.com/Olivia-Fox/e/B07ZXMH4CN

Don't miss my other **naughty ever after** books about alpha males, Daddy Doms and stories with spank. Not to mention the smart and sassy heroines who love them.

ALL BOOKS ARE **FREE** ON KINDLE UNLIMITED.

LOST COAST DADDIES ROMANCE SERIES

Sizzling Hot Daddy
Daddy's Sweet Ride
Daddy's Law
Lost Coast Daddies Romance Box Set
Daddy's Little Wild One
Daddy's Pet

Dirty Fairy Tale Series - Demanding Daddy

Captured - A Beauty and the Beast retelling
Claimed - A Little Mermaid retelling
Ravished - A Little Red Riding Hood retelling

***Claimed*: Deep-sea diver left for dead.**

A speechless siren finds him on the deserted strand. A guy who battles sharks, near drowning, and oozes danger.
Eric García
The waves of fate tossed him up on the shores of my solitude, and for the first time since the collision, I feel safe.
A man who swims in the ocean depths, fearing nothing. Mentally and physically fit. He wants me to use my words. Why would he understand that I've stayed protected from the heartlessness of humans only by remaining here on the abandoned shore of the Pacific Ocean? Hiding. Silent.

He's rough. Bold. And insists that I call him "daddy". But how can I when a horrible incident took my words away forever?

Beneath the steely surface lies a devoted and gentle heart that I don't want to disappoint - one that needs to claim me as his.

No way am I going back to village with him so he can spoil me like he says I deserve. Even though his firm hand and punishments make me squirm, in a good way, this won't work.

I'm an unusual girl, twenty years his junior, who earns her living selling shellfish. The laughingstock of Bryarville. Eric doesn't know about the deal I sealed for my aunt's silence - an arrangement I'd ruin by showing my face in town.

His kisses set off a sharp, wild need in me, and I hope that mine tell him without speech that I love him.

He demands that I'm his. But I fear this desire burning between us won't survive the ugly that flourishes where the people are.

From Amazon Best Seller: Olivia Fox comes this age gap, alpha romance. Claimed is part of her Dirty Fairy Tales series, inspired by The Little Mermaid. Each book is a stand-alone, naughty ever after.

♥ If you crave scorchingly, steamy stories, scroll up and click the button to buy. ♥

◆This book does not feature age play, pacis or Pull-Ups®. It features a significant age gap.◆

***Ravished*: A real, live mountain man.**

Zeke Midas.

A tasty morsel of a lumberjack at that.

He's an axe-wielding tree feller, plain-spoken and burly. Back in high school, he barely knew I existed except for our weekly tutoring sessions. It pains me to admit it, I've never encountered a man yummier than him.

Now we're both grown up, and he tells me it's time to feed the wolf. That I'm the first and only female to speak to the animal he keeps hidden away.

I'm not so sure about that.

Zeke isn't the only male to make my hormones sing, but he's the only man I can't forget.

So what is it between us?

Hormones, or happy ever after?

Every night he lays me bare, looking into my eyes as he takes me to the abyss, and shows me the darkest, most depraved secrets inside me. Somehow he knows more about what I want than I do myself. The things he reveals to me... they're obscene, scandalous...

I can't get enough of them.

When he tells me he needs me. I realize I have to get away. Otherwise, he's going to pull me into the powerful dark side with him forever, and show me once and for all what my wicked body is made for.

Zeke is the wolf: a bad boy who likes to get his hands dirty. And just like that dark villain, he can see me better, hear me better and eat me better.

The question is, am I ready?

★ From Amazon Best Seller: Olivia Fox comes this mountain man, friends to lovers, alpha romance. *Ravished* is part of her Dirty Fairy Tales series, inspired by *Little Red Riding Hood,* in the Demanding Daddy Series. Each book is a standalone, naughty ever after. Transport yourself into the charming and magical town of Briarville and beyond. Follow these commanding yet gentle heros on their quests to find lasting love and naughtiness on the real live Lost Coast of California. ★

www.ingramcontent.com/pod-product-compliance
Lightning Source LLC
Chambersburg PA
CBHW061219210726
48294CB00006B/1906